Man of Smoke

Man of Smoke

Aldo Palazzeschi

Translated from the Italian
with an introduction by
Nicolas J. Perella and Ruggero Stefanini

ITALICA PRESS
NEW YORK
1992

ITALICA PRESS, INC.
595 Main Street
New York, New York 10044

Library of Congress Cataloging-in-Publication Data

Palazzeschi, Aldo, 1885-1974.
[Codice di Perelà. English]
Man of smoke / by Aldo Palazzeschi ; translated from the Italian
with an introduction by Nicolas J. Perella and Ruggero Stefanini.
    p.   cm.
Translation of: Il codice di Perelà.
Includes bibliographies.
ISBN 0-934977-26-7 : $14.95
I. Perella, Nicolas J. (Nicolas James), 1927-   . II. Stefanini,
Ruggero, 1932-   . III. Title.
PQ4835.A18C63613   1992
853'.912--dc20   92-1240
                                                  CIP

Printed in the United States of America
5 4 3 2 1

Cover art: "The Introvert" © 1992 by Margaret McCann

Major Works of Aldo Palazzeschi

Prose

:riflessi (:reflections), 1908

Il codice di Perelà, romanzo futurista (The Code of Perelà, A Futurist Novel), 1911; *Il codice di Perelà*, 1920; published as *Perelà uomo di fumo* (Perelà, Man of Smoke) in 1954

Due imperi...mancati (Two Failed Empires), 1920

Il re bello (The Handsome King), 1920

La Piramide (The Pyramid), 1926

Stampe dell'800 (Nineteenth-Century Lithographs), 1932

Sorelle Materassi (The Materassi Sisters), 1934

Il palio dei buffi (The Parade of the *Buffi*), 1937, 1944

I fratelli Cuccoli (The Cuccoli Brothers), 1948

Bestie del 900 (Twentieth-Century Animals), 1951

Roma, 1953

Scherzi di gioventù (Youthful Pranks), 1956

Il piacere della memoria (The Pleasures of Memory), 1964

Il buffo integrale (The Complete *Buffo*), 1966

Il Doge (The Doge), 1967

Stefanino, 1969

Storia di un'amicizia (Story of a Friendship), 1971

Poetry

I cavalli bianchi (White Horses), 1905

Lanterna (Lantern), 1907

Poemi (Poems), 1909

L'incendiario (The Arsonist), 1910, 1913

Poesie (Poems), 1925

Viaggio sentimentale (Sentimental Journey), 1955

Cuor mio (Heart of Mine), 1968

Via delle cento stelle (Street of a Hundred Stars), 1972

Sinfonie (Symphonies), posthumous

About the Translators

Nicolas J. Perella was born in Boston, MA. He received a B.A. from Suffolk University and an M.A. and a Ph.D. in Romance Languages from Harvard University. He has been on the faculty of the University of California at Berkeley since 1957.

Ruggero Stefanini was born and educated in Italy. He received his doctoral degree from the University of Florence and has been on the faculty of the University of California at Berkeley since 1961.

Contents

Introduction

> There is a lightness of thoughtfulness, just as
> we all know that there is a lightness of fri-
> volity. In fact, thoughtful lightness can make
> frivolity seem heavy and dull.
>
> – Italo Calvino, "Lightness"

Palazzeschi's Life and Works

Of Italy's major twentieth-century writers, perhaps the least known to the English-speaking world
is Aldo Palazzeschi. Aldo Giurlani (Palazzeschi,
his nom de plume, was in reality the family name of
his maternal grandmother) was born in Florence in
1885, the only child of a well-to-do merchant who
owned a chic haberdashery in the elegant Via dei
Calzaioli. Following grammar school, the young
Aldo attended the Istituto Tecnico where he was
trained as a future accountant. But his interests
were elsewhere, and while still in his teens, he enrolled in a famous school for acting, soon joining
the touring company of Virgilio Talli. After a few
performances, however, he gave up the stage and
returned to Florence where, at his own expense, he
had already published a slim volume of poems, *I
cavalli bianchi.*

From then on, thanks also to the fact that he had
an independent income, he dedicated himself to a
literary career, which in its early years did not
bring him much recognition. Until 1913 he wrote
both poetry and prose. In addition to two novels –
:riflessi and *Il codice di Perelà* – he published his
poems in several volumes: *Lanterna, Poemi,* and
L'incendiario. In this period Palazzeschi associated
himself with F. T. Marinetti's Futurist movement

and contributed to avant-garde periodicals and a raging literary polemic. Although a pacifist by nature and persuasion, he served in the Italian army (though never in combat) during World War I. At the war's end, back in Florence he devoted himself to writing novels, short stories, and memoirs in a style that gradually departed from the fantastic inventiveness of his earlier work. It was perhaps also because of this more accessible manner (allegedly "naturalistic") that he won considerable success, particularly with *Stampe dell'800* and *Sorelle Materassi.*

During the '20s and '30s, he spent extended periods in Paris. At the beginning of World War II, Palazzeschi, whose parents had recently died, moved to Rome where, with the exception of stays in Paris and Venice, he lived until his death. His activity as a novelist brought him two coveted literary prizes, one for *I fratelli Cuccoli* in 1948 and the other for *Roma* in 1953. The publication of *Il Doge* in 1967 signalled a prodigious return of youth for the octogenarian author. Not only did he write two more novels *(Stefanino* and *Storia di un'amicizia)* in which, as in *Il Doge,* the uninhibited imagination that characterized his early works triumphs, but after decades of writing exclusively in prose, he astonished the Italian literary world with his rediscovery of poetry: *Cuor mio* and *Via delle cento stelle,* and the posthumously published *Sinfonie.*

Palazzeschi, who had enjoyed excellent health throughout his long life, died in Rome in August 1974 from complications connected with an abscessed tooth. In accordance with his last will, he was buried in Settignano, a small hill town near Florence. His library and papers were bequeathed to the University of Florence.

Palazzeschi and the Critics

For those beyond Italy's frontier who have heard
of Palazzeschi, the name often brings to mind not
one of the century's most radically innovative narrative masterpieces, *Il codice di Perelà,* but rather
one, or at most two, of his novels, in particular
Sorelle Materassi, written in a fairly traditional
mode. Literary critics today may not hesitate to
number the experimental 1911 anti-novel, here
translated *Man of Smoke,* among the most original
books of modern fiction – a work to be set
alongside Svevo's *La coscienza di Zeno* and the best
of Pirandello's theater. But it was not always so.

Its appearance in 1911 was hailed by the Italian
avant-garde and certain young radicals among the
intelligentsia of Florence intent on shaking up the
provincial and rhetorical character of Italy's pre-
vailing middle-class culture. However, the few
leading critics who reviewed it did so with knitted
brows. Despite four later editions (each one
revised to a greater or lesser degree) during the
author's lifetime, *Man of Smoke* failed to achieve
the critical acclaim it deserved. The rise to its
present high ranking began only in the late 50s,
when the great swell of post-World War II neo-
realism had abated sufficiently to allow another
look around.

At the time he was writing the first version of
Man of Smoke, between 1908 and 1910, Palazzeschi enjoyed a modicum of notoriety as a writer of
verse in two veins. One is characterized by a
dreamy, enigmatic, fairy-tale atmosphere (suggesting a link with the art nouveau style and the Franco-
Belgian symbolists), a subdued tone and a
deceptive simplicity of language. Not without
some irony and mischievousness, the whole is
dominated by a sense of loneliness, of transgression

and castigation, of a culprit/victim complex, of a repressed sexuality and an occasional sadomasochistic touch.

The other vein, introduced warily in the 1909 volume *Poemi,* is marked by irreverent parodic play in which the concealed or closeted self begins to break free with exhibitionistic nose thumbing, even taking over some of the thematic repertory of the earlier volumes and reworking it into the new manner. It was this latter vein that won the admiration of Italy's flamboyant founder of Futurism, F. T. Marinetti, who quickly enrolled the Florentine poet in his revolutionary coterie. Marinetti even sponsored the publication of a volume of Palazzeschi's poems, as well as the first edition of *Man of Smoke.*

The Style of Man of Smoke

One of the formal revolutionary aspects of *Man of Smoke,* the work Palazzeschi always referred to as his "aerial fairy tale," is its extraordinary theatricalization of the novel. Of the eighteen "chapters," only a handful are strictly narrative. The majority, for all practical purposes, are scenes, with some combining scene and a concise present-tense narration whose style is often that of "on-the-scene" reportage or written stage directions.

Dialog and direct discourse, without a guiding authorial voice, is often used to advance the story line, as at the novel's very opening. One thinks of Manuel Puig's *The Kiss of the Spider Woman* and other modern novels written mainly in quotation marks. Such direct discourse is also used "chorally," with anonymous individual voices of a group or crowd uttering observations in a single brief sentence or even in a single exclamatory or interrogative word. The effect is sometimes like the dazzling patter of a Rossinian *opera buffa.* In the few well-chosen moments when Palazzeschi takes personal command as the narrating voice, he remains unconventional, playfully mimicking different genres and styles, even the language of grammar-school readers.

Though *Man of Smoke* does without the time-out-of-time *incipit* "Once upon a time," a reader will not mistake the nature of its surrealistic, fairy-tale atmosphere. Within this atmosphere, besides blithely introducing anachronisms such as telephones, photographers, cigarettes, etc. (and perhaps because of them), Palazzeschi is able to set his satire of modern society and human nature in general. His use of the classic fairy-tale mode can be traced from some of his early poems, where it figures as a "content" somewhat morbidly longed for in an estheticizing reverie, to *Man of Smoke,* where it functions as an ironic (and paradoxical) metaphor of existence and of the world as a farcical penitentiary. The process is perfectly realized in the novel thanks to the necessity of a story line, however tenuous, which the dreamy, mystifying tableaux of the poems could do without.

There is something analogous here to the wonderful amalgamation of and interplay between fairy tale and realism found in Collodi's *Adventures of Pinocchio* (1881-83). In one case the protagonist is a boy made out of wood, in the other a man made out of smoke. Wood, however, is a material substance and therefore has weight, though in Collodi's hands it dances, runs, and leaps ever so airily. Smoke is, in more than one sense, the essence of insubstantiality. Perelà is smoke compacted into a human form, but his compactness is without density. While he is a puppet-boy of wood (i.e., a hyperkinetic marionette), Pinocchio is intent on escaping from any confinement or regimentation that restricts his desire for uninhibited pleasure. His story is replete with episodes and images (including actual imprisonment) having to do with shackling him. At the end, in a self-betrayal dictated by the author's need to bend his irreverent puppet to a bourgeois moral, the metamorphosed Pinocchio, now a real and all too priggish boy, scornfully looks at the wooden marionette he once was with the words "How funny I was when I was a puppet; and how glad I am now that I have become a proper boy," not realizing that it is he who is now the real puppet, sworn to the law-and-order conformity demanded by society.

Man of Smoke will have no part of so abject a resignation. But both Pinocchio before his metamorphosis and Perelà are symbols of the liberating force of the imagination, of fantasy, which is always potentially explosive. And it is from the initial ambiguity of their dual natures that there stems an endless chain of possible ironies, consciously exploited by their respective creators. Hence, it can come as no surprise that, in the hands of an author who seldom loses the opportunity to turn a linguistic joke, a man of smoke should have a plurality of meanings, contradictory if one likes, but not mutually exclusive. Laughter and comedy have their own logic, as do dreams and fairy tales; and ambiguity is of their essence.

It is a pity that in his essay on "Lightness," Italo Calvino makes no mention of Palazzeschi either in thematic or stylistic terms, for there is no doubt that the author of *The Cloven Viscount, The Nonexistent Knight,* and even of *The Castle of Crossed Destinies,* was influenced by *Man of Smoke.* But certainly no other work of modern fiction, not even Milan Kundera's much later *The Unbearable Lightness of Being* (which Calvino does touch on), so programmatically takes as its central existential theme the tragicomic play on the opposition between lightness and heaviness.

Perelà, the Queen, and God

The existential nature of Palazzeschi's tale is coded into the very name of its protagonist. Let us not forget that the novel's Italian title in all editions but one is *The Code of Perelà;* and in the one exception, *Perelà, Man of Smoke* (1954), the protagonist's name still appears. In a book rich with paradoxes, the chief paradox is its oxymoronic antihero: a man of smoke. The name given so frivolously to him by the gentlemen of the Court who have listened to the account he gives of his difficult birth, a name that sounds so trippingly on the tongue, is compounded from the first syllable of each of the names of the three centenarians Perelà considers his mothers – a triune mother or a feminine trinity: *Pe[na]* (Pain), *Re[te]* (Net), *La[ma]* (Blade). The words, which bespeak the acrid taste of existence, will be glossed existentially by the Queen, as by a sibyl. It is worth noting, then, that the Queen is the only figure in the novel who escapes Palazzeschi's irony or humor. Indeed, in her opening remarks to Perelà at the private audience granted him, the Queen may be said to identify herself with the man of smoke and his triune mother:

> Like you, Perelà, I think of those three women. I am at the top of a chimney and I hear them talking....They talk of human suffering. Of the three who is speaking? Is it *Pena?* Is it *Rete?* Is it *Lama?* One tells of a heart's pain. One spreads the net that ensnared it. One carries in her hand the blade that will pierce it.

Thus, by dissecting this seemingly *opera buffa* sort of name (Perelà), the tragic trilogy of life is brought to the fore.

If the Marchesa di Bellonda is a burlesqued but *simpatica* Mary Magdalen, believing in and devoted to Perelà, the Queen is formed on the Marian archetype of the *mater dolorosa,* invested with the mantle of universal grief, but pure and gentle at the same time. Near the end of the novel, when Perelà is marched out of the city to his solitary prison cell, the unidentified white face that appears momentarily in the window of the stationary carriage is certainly hers.

Although the Queen herself is not ironized, Palazzeschi is able, remarkably, to make her one of three players in a precarious scene – *her* scene – that reduces God to a meaningless word. Human pain naturally turns to God for comfort and justification. During their conversation the Queen's parrot is intermittently heard interjecting the single word "God." While the parrot does not know the meaning of this "greatest word of all," Perelà suggests that the Queen at least knows. But her reply begins with assurance only to end hesitantly and inconclusively. What we may be left to assume is that parrots cannot possibly know what the word "God" means, while people reassure themselves by pretending to know, when in fact they may know no more than parrots do.

The word left unsaid by the Queen will be spoken later by someone who need not be reticent about even the most taboo of subjects. An inmate of the madhouse visited by Perelà puts the question to which he himself gives an answer that also implicates the man of smoke: "Don't you know what God is? God is everything and God is nothing: for the perfection created by humankind cannot be anything other than nothing. They decided to give a name to nothingness, and thereby they made it become something. Like you, you are still something. Smoke is not nothing, it is smoke; just so, God, who is nothingness, can no longer be nothing, since he is God." One is led to wonder whether Palazzeschi was making parodic use of the Johannine gospel's stunning exordium ("In the beginning was the Word, and the Word was with God, and the Word was God") and also of the haunting one-word refrain of Poe's raven.

Palazzeschi's protagonist is a most singular oxymoron, almost as singular as the divine oxymoron Christ (true God and true man, spirit and matter) of which he is a parody. The very essence of lightness and insubstantiality (i.e., of nothingness), and the absolute image of otherness, the man of smoke is the novel's central metaphor. Hailed as a savior by the society into which he has descended, he is entrusted with the weighty task of prescribing a new Civil Code, a New Testament, as it were. Perelà does not say, as does the tramp in Samuel Beckett's *Waiting for Godot,* "All my life I have compared myself with Christ." But the parodic *imitatio Christi* is evident enough. Like Christ, he issues from a womb unfertilized by man's seed. He is thirty-three years old. And like Christ he will undergo a *passio,* an entombment, and an ascent; but it will be in a tragicomic key, and the ascent will be a final escape and dissolution into airy nothingness.

Yet the man of smoke, though a metaphor of the nothingness of humanity, is also a metaphor of the pain of existence. The Code he is expected to write, but which could never be written, is the novel's "absent" structure, the fulcrum or pivot of the story line, forever elusive.

Perelà and Palazzeschi

The reader may or may not wish to see Perelà also as a metaphor for Palazzeschi's homosexuality. There are indeed several implied or indirect allusions to it, starting with the book's opening – an exchange of dialog. Perelà's apparently naive question to the first person he meets: "Would you be a man, by chance?" is answered really with an ironic jibe: "No. I'm a poor old woman; you're probably a man by chance." Perelà later says: "I'm light...a light man...very, very light," where "light" could also mean "gay" in more than its primary sense. And in the chapter "The Tea," in addition to an occasional snide insinuation one or two of them make regarding Perelà's manhood, the ladies of high society feel perfectly safe in telling him in lurid detail the stories of their intimate sex lives.

But it would be perverse to read *Man of Smoke* too closely as an autobiographical allegory. Palazzeschi's homosexuality (perhaps never actively practised), along with an ambiguous nostalgia for "normality," and the sense of loneliness, of alienation and of imprisonment that accompanied it, contributed to making him a better sounding board for a more universal sense of alienation. Homosexuality is not treated directly by him, and Perelà as the metaphor for the author's homosexuality acquires aesthetic and human relevance in the novel only insofar as homosexuality itself becomes a metaphor for the pain of existence. To be "a man by chance" suggests tragicomically the cruel hoax played by the absurd fortuitousness of existence.

Palazzeschi, fortunately, could laugh above the pain at anything absurd. He could also see more of the absurd than most of us. Paradoxically, the weightless protagonist is a metaphor for the heaviness, that is, the pain, of existence. But, oxymoron that he is, he is also the symbol of lightness, that is, the liberating force of laughter (though he himself never laughs) and the poetic imagination.

The Code

That a man of smoke should be entrusted with so weighty a task as that of creating a new Civil Code is all due to a misunderstanding that reveals the ineptitude of presumably wise men. After ponderously considering Perelà's account of his birth, the notables of the Court decide that "he is the man whom the purifying flame enveloped so as to annihilate the turbid travail and dross of matter," the man sent by Divine Providence to establish "a just measure (i.e., the new Code) by which to weigh and judge the conscience of each of us." But if Perelà can rightly be considered, in the words of the Minister, "a sublimation of the body and the human spirit," it is not in a bourgeois and Philistine sense. It is, rather, in the sense of a congenital freedom and an ambivalent detachment that the Minister and the others can perceive only in the negative terms of subversion and anarchy. When this is suspected, following the grotesque suicide by fire of the old Palace servant Alloro (who presumed to become by art what one can be only by nature or, if one prefers, "by chance," i.e., a man of smoke), Perelà's fortunes are reversed.

In the meantime, before going into seclusion to formulate the new Code, the man of smoke, who started life with an optimistic and romanticized outlook, will be led on a guided tour of society's institutions. This and the events that subsequently befall him will turn what remains of his naive optimism into bitter wisdom. In point of fact, this process of disenchantment and enlightenment and the first accents of a bitter melancholy that courses through this genuinely funny book, date from Perelà's initial contact with the real world. War and love are the first myths to fall from the shock of recognition, with an irony that invests not only the protagonist but his creator as well. From the readings and conversation of his triune mother, Perelà had pictured war as a goreless, joyously winged ballet, and love as an image of floreate gossamer. Visions, that is, in terms suggestive of Maeterlink and *art nouveau,* but now in an ironic key, for the first impressions he receives reveal war and love to be something nauseously thick and viscous: the grayish soup of heavy artillery (war) and the pot filled with the yellowish organic waste that an old bawd secretively pours into a black crevice (love).

The Romantic "Buffo"
It is by a deliberate irony that *Man of Smoke,* an apparently anti-romantic book, turns on what is the central theme of Romanticism – the clash between the real and the ideal. But we can already see that in developing the theme Palazzeschi adopts a strategy for satire not unlike the one much used in the eighteenth century of placing a foreign visitor in a great metropolis where he records observations on the customs and institutions of a "strange" society. Montesquieu's *Lettres persanes* comes to mind of course, but so does the closely related strategy familiar to us in Voltaire's *Candide.* In many ways Perelà is both a foreigner par excellence (a stranger in a strange land who has come from "up there," which is essentially nowhere) and an ingenu, albeit one that Palazzeschi uses wittily to confound and deflate the learned and the civilized.

A stranger and an ingenu, on first appearing among humans – before he is acclaimed as a messianic figure – Perelà is twice referred to by others

as a *"tipo buffo."* A translator is hard put to choose
among the several words available for *buffo:* odd,
queer, weird, strange, comical, funny, droll, laugh-
able, ridiculous, ludicrous, etc. Certainly, from the
perspective of "normal" human beings, Perelà is a
"funny" character in the two meanings of the word:
strange and comical, to use the most neutral terms
in the list. Nonetheless, one feels that "funny" is
not quite right. Fortunately, we have a definition of
the term from the writer himself that allows us to
use the Italian word while suggesting a psycho-
logical dimension that will keep us from confusing
it with the term as used in an operatic context:

> *Buffi* are all those persons who, because of
> some [peculiar] trait, or natural divergence of
> various kinds, writhe in discomfiture amidst
> the general community of humans. This dis-
> comfiture assumes at one and the same time
> tones of heightened comedy and deep gloom.

Now, Perelà is undoubtedly a congenital *buffo,*
one might even say a freak. But for a good part of
the novel, while he is the honored guest of the
Court and then Inspector General of the State, it is
not he who appears to be so. In fact, it is the others
who make up a variegated gallery of *buffi* and gro-
tesques. In a reversal of the roles assigned at the
beginning, Perelà the gazing-stock becomes the
spectator; and the supposed spectators, though they
partially retain that function, become the laughing-
stocks. The roles will be turned around again in the
last part of the novel, when the spotlight will be
focused on a disgraced Perelà, and the dominant,
but not the only, tone will be the tragic/pathetic.
The man of smoke is a *buffo* moving in a world of
buffi.

As a stranger/ingenu in a strange land, Perelà does little talking; his role is to listen and sometimes inquire as to the whys and wherefores of things. Understandably he is most loquacious in the first chapter, where, once inside the Royal Palace, his replies to the Master of Ceremonies make for a circumstantial narrative of his birth, nature, and provenance, an account his listeners (mis)interpret as they please. It is as though he had spoken monologues, as he did in fact shortly before in his reflections on war and love. Thereafter, he will be a man of few words – brief, pointed questions and interpolations – until the monologue that is his disabused farewell to earth.

Having become a celebrity, with greatness thrust upon him *malgré lui*, Perelà is besieged by those who wish to see, touch, and speak to him. The innate and apparently unconscious subversiveness of the man of smoke is evident in all the interviews. With a few well-chosen and well-placed words, Perelà can be a veritable lord of misrule. Even when he is completely silent (as in "The Tea"), his mere presence has a catalytic effect.

Palazzeschi's Tragicomedy

"Existence itself, the act of existing, is a striving, and is both pathetic and comic in the same degree." Kierkegaard's statement, as much as and more than Palazzeschi's definition of his *buffi*, defines the tragicomic drama of Perelà. It is symptomatic that the character with whom Perelà (and Palazzeschi) has the greatest affinity is Prince Zarlino, the voluntary or "conscious" lunatic. Zarlino's self-commitment to the madhouse is a rejection of society; but his ambiguous lunacy is, or borders on, actual madness (though, paradoxically, madness is seen as a liberation). The slightest slip would find him violently strapped down by the asylum's attendants. Here one can hardly avoid thinking of Pirandello and his own gallery of *buffi*, among whom is Henry IV. Concerning Perelà specifically, however, another author contemporary to Palazzeschi might also rightly come to mind. If one does not stretch the matter too far, a parallel can be drawn between *Man of Smoke* and Franz Kafka's novels. It is true, of course, that Perelà, unlike Kafka's heroes, is a curiously inert victim, but insofar as he does seek, however unwittingly, for an identity or a place among humans and ingenuously wishes to belong to their world, he shares a common existential fate with the protagonists of *The Trial* (1914) and *The Castle* (1922), moving as a total outsider in a world that has become wholly hostile to him.

The tragicomic play on the lightness-weight opposition reaches its climax in the three successive chapters, beginning with "Why?," where the dominant tone is a lyrical pathos, and ending with "The Trial of Perelà," a farce in a technical and figurative sense, as grotesque and nightmarish in its ludic fashion as any lived by Kafka's protagonists. And finally, the last words of Perelà's monologue are a despondent allusion to the world's failure to understand his lightness. Now, as he releases himself into the blue of nothingness, Perelà finishes his monologue and his earthly sojourn.

But any danger *Man of Smoke* may have run of ending in an indulgence of self-pity over the acrid taste of existence is averted by its last chapter (one page!), where all pathos and any suggestion of nihilism are dissipated in an ironic and vitalistic laugh. Even after several readings, this last page, wholly in direct discourse, may seem to be an enigmatic anticlimax or a surprising palinode. Yet it is perfectly in keeping with the book's overall tone and spirit. The anonymous voices evidently come from couples of lovers (perhaps those in the Meadow of Love) engaged in their irrational and happy play. They too would like to fly to meet those festive clouds they see above and which they fantasize as "new men," eagles, and banners.

What Palazzeschi suggests here is that the absurd yet wonderful spectacle of life goes on, freely reinvented by each new generation with gusto and above all with love. For as Palazzeschi will affectionately reassure us in a poem of his old age, life and poetry go hand in hand along an endless road filled with unpredictable adventures. Over time and space they are both infinite. The peal of laughter heard in the last line of *Man of Smoke* is the triumph of joy: *Allegrìa!*

Select Critical Bibliography

Alessandri, Luca. "Assenza e identità nel Codice di Perelà di Palazzeschi," *Lingua e stile* 24 (1989): 115-48.

Curi, Fausto. "'Buffo,' parodia, utopia." In *Parodia e Utopia*. Naples: Liguori editore, 1987, pp. 127-58.

Dei, Adele. "Note e Postfazione." In *Lanterna* by A. Palazzeschi. Parma: Edizioni Zara, 1987.

De Maria, Luciano. "Introduzione." In *Il Codice di Perela* by A. Palazzeschi. Milan: Mondadori, 1974, pp. vii-xvi.

Gugliemi, Guido. *L'udienza del poeta: Saggi su Palazzeschi e il futurismo*. Turin: Einaudi, 1979.

Lugnani, L. "La prima raccolta di Palazzeschi," *Linguistica e letteratura* 8,1 (1983): 81-151.

Memmo, Francesco Paolo. *Invito alla lettura di Palazzeschi*. Milan: Mursia editore, 1976.

Palazzeschi oggi. Ed. by L. Caretti. Conference Proceedings, Florence, November 6-8, 1976. Milan: Il Saggiatore, 1978.

Pieri, Piero. *Ritratto del saltimbanco da giovane: Palazzeschi 1905-1914*. Bologna: Patròn editore, 1980.

Saccone, Antonio. *L'occhio narrante: tre studi sul primo Palazzeschi*. Naples: Liguori, 1987.

Saccone, Eduardo. "*Alleg(o)ria di Novembre*: La sublimazione imperfetta di Aldo Palazzeschi," *Modern Language Notes* 92,1 (1977): 79-116.

Tamburri, Anthony Julian. *Of Saltimbanchi and Incendiari: Aldo Palazzeschi and Avant-Gardism in Italy*. Rutherford, NJ: Fairleigh Dickinson University Press, London: Associated University Presses, 1990.

Man of Smoke

The Black Uterus

Pena! [Pain] *Rete!* [Net] *Lama!* [Blade] *Pena!*
Rete! Lama! Pe...Re...La...
  – Would you be a man, by chance?
  – No. I'm a poor old woman, you're probably a man by chance.
  – Quite so, quite so, forgive me, you're right. You're a poor old woman, I'm a man.
  – Just what are you?
  – I'm light...a light man...very, very light...and you're a poor old woman, I know, like *Pena;* like *Rete,* like *Lama;* they, too, were old women. Could you tell me if what I see at the end of this road is the city?
  – It is.
  – Then what I see down there is very likely the King's residence?
  – No, that's the city gate and the city walls. The King's residence is located in the middle of a garden; it's encircled by a very high iron fence and is carefully guarded by the police. The citizens there often kill their King. Now Torlindao is King. But are you headed for the city, sir?
  – Yes.
  – You'll soon be there. And where are you from?
  – From up there.
  – They've never seen you in the city?
  – I'm going there for the first time.
  – Look there, look at that cloud of dust coming towards us; it's the King's brigade, the mounted police, they're coming to patrol the outskirts of the city. I'm leaving. Goodby, sir, goodby, seeing me

1

with you they might become suspicious. If they
question you, watch how you answer, they're quick
to become suspicious, and you're apt to attract
their attention. A safe journey to you, goodby.

– Did you see how we covered him with dust?
you could no longer tell what he was.
– When we got close to him, I thought I saw him
disappear.
– It's true, so did I.
– But that wasn't a man at all, you know!
– What was it then? *You* tell us.
– It looked like a cloud.
– Of course, we covered him with dust.
– We're the ones who look like a cloud, on this
damn road!
– No, no, I saw him before the road became
thick with dust, he's a man of smoke!
– Blockhead!
– Idiot!
– Are you kidding, a man of smoke? You've got it
wrong, it must be a jackass roast.
– I got a good look at his boots.
– He's wearing polished boots, the kind our
officers wear.
– I say he's a knight of old.
– Hold up for a moment.
– Why don't we turn back?
– What for?
– At least to see him, to question him, one never
knows...
– I'm not taking a step without a good reason.
– Shall we make a bet?
– Bet what?
– Whatever you want.

– A pair of boots like those of your jackass of old, a jackass of the latest style.

Pena! Rete! Lama! Pena! Rete! Lama! Pe...Re...La...
– Hey, my good man, where are you going?
– Over there.
– That's a good one. Would you mind telling us just what in the world you are?
– I'm...very much...very...a man. Yes, a man.
– You're not much of a man; it seems to me that the only thing of a man about you are your boots.
– Where are you from?
– From up there.
– That's a good one, too. Say, my good man, do you know whom you're talking to?
– To the King's brigade.
– Thank goodness. Well then you must know that it's dangerous to fool with us.
– Ask him what he's made of.
– You ask him, stupid.
– What are you made of, sir?
– I'm very...so very...so very light.
– What I meant was: what substance is your body made of?
– Smoke.
– There! I told you so. He's a man of smoke, a man of smoke! Smoke! Smoke! Smoke!
– Quiet, brat, or I'll send *you* up in smoke.
– But he's right!
– After all, why be stubborn?
– Can't we all see?
– Isn't it obvious?
– Smoke! Smoke! Smoke!
– Shut up, I said!

– But no, it's true, he's right.
– You're all worried about your bet.
– How beautiful those boots are!
– And how shiny they are!
– I've never seen a pair of boots like that.
– What a shine!
– A mirror!
– Be quiet, you guys, I've already told you once.
– But why, since it's true?
– Smoke! Smoke! Smoke!
– You can see right away...
– At first sight.
– Shall we go and tell the King?
– Let's go and tell the King.
– Let's go, yes, let's go.
– Right, he may want to see him.
– Who knows what he'll say!
– A man of smoke!
– Smoke! Smoke! Smoke!
– Will you shut up, blast it all!
– Smoke! Smoke! Smoke!

Pena! Rete! Lama! Pena! Rete! Lama!
Pe...Re...La...
– No duty to pay, sir? Don't act dumb, friend.
Have you got anything? Inside your boots?
– I am...so very light.
– My dear sir, there are extremely light things
for which a duty tax must be paid. With your boots
you could cheat the government.
– What a queer duck!
– Did you see what a strange color?
– The color of fog, dear chap, a sign that the
weather is going to change.
– No!

4

– What's wrong?
– I've figured it out.
– What?
– He's made out of smoke!
– Ha! Ha! Ha! Ha!
– Yes he's made out of smoke!
– Hey, just listen to this, he saw a man of smoke go by!
– Absolutely!
– Ha! Ha! Ha! Ha!
– And how much duty did you make him pay? It's not included in our table of charges.
– What characters, the both of you!
– I can assure all of you, it can't be otherwise; he himself declared he felt so very light. I looked at him close up.
– Ha! Ha! Ha! Ha!

– Are you a man?
– Of course.
– Can you tell me who that is? Is he a man, too?
– Certainly, a soldier. He's ready for war.
– War?
– Don't you see how laden he is with steel, iron, and lead? He's a soldier, naturally.
– War...steel...iron...lead...but aren't such things awfully heavy?
– Certainly. You can't attack the enemy with candy. And you, what are you?
– I am...very, very light, a very light man.
– What a character!

– How many times I have heard this word: war. *Pena, Rete, Lama,* they always spoke of war, and I imagined that men ran naked to war, that they removed even their footwear so that their steps would be nimble and silent like those of a leopard, so light that they could hurtle through the air with unexpected and stealthy leaps in order to sneak up, to hide, to steal away...I saw them snatching wings from birds putting them to use as weapons. Steel... iron...lead....And aren't they crushed under so much weight? How can they swiftly attack the enemy, or slip quickly away when attacked? And I saw fields marked by red blood, as if those men had freed themselves of it so as to run more lightly and proclaim their victory. Now I see war as an enormous gray soup dished out with a long low din, and left there...inedible.

    – Ho, there!
    – Sir!
    – Hurry, sir!
    – You too!
    – Hurry, quick!
    – Help!
    – Lend us a hand!
    – Help! Help!
    – Look!
    – Come!
    – Do you see this well? Come closer. Look down there. Two girls just lowered themselves down there, and we can't pull them out.
    – They're probably dead by now.
    – Help us, for pity's sake!
    – They say this well has no bottom.
    – That's great!
    – How beautiful they were!
    – Their eyes were heavenly stars!
    – Their curls were blacker than a raven's wings!

– And their mouths seemed like coral jewel-boxes filled with pearls!

– They seemed born to hail the dawn!

– Because of love!

– They decided to kill themselves!

– Both were in love with the same man!

– To the point of ruin!

– To the point of suicide!

– He's over there, weeping, rolling on the ground; his mother is holding him, otherwise he too would have jumped into the well.

– Two maidens from Venice!

– They had come here to string pearls for the Queen and all the ladies of the Court.

– And because of love they decided to cut short their days.

– They loved the same man?

– Yes, sir.

– And why did they throw themselves into the well?

– Good heavens, because they were unhappy! How could he, with only one heart, requite two such burning hearts?

– But then only one of them should have jumped in.

– Keep quiet, what do you know about such things?

– Who are you?

– Only one of them! What a nerve!

– Send him away! Make him go away!

– Can't you see he's a queer duck?

– He must not even be a man.

– What can he be?

– A bad sort, that's what he is!

– He's not a man! He's not a man!

– He's a thick cloud that's come down very low!
– Phooey! He's wearing a cloak of lead.
– Yes, he's a man, but he's dressed in an elephant skin.
– Look at those beautiful boots!
– He stole them, he stole them from someplace, you can be sure he stole them!

– Love! How many times I have heard this word rise up to me and enter my breast. I remember *Pena, Rete, Lama* when they spoke this word. Their voices would become tremulous and uncertain, as though on the verge of going aloft in the air, like the move- ment of tiny birds in their nest at the first vital itch, when still unaware they sense their wings and their flights. Love. And I would see two golden-haired creatures, draped in extremely light, diaphanous robes, pink and blue, looking into one another's face with a pure joy and rising up into the air, in a halo of white wings, borne by a cloud of flowers. Down there...at the very bottom of that dark well...while he's over there writhing about in the dust...because of a threesome in love....Now I see an old hag with wan skin, wrinkled, all wrapped in a black shawl threadbare and greenish with age. She is kneeling and holds a red-clay pot in her hand; surly, wary, she turns around, so that nobody catches her pouring some yellow liquid into a black crevice in the earth.

– Come in, come in, sir!
– Come up, the Grand Master of Ceremonies awaits you, surrounded by all the noblemen.
– Sir, in the name of the King, the Queen and the entire Court, I welcome you as guest of the Royal

Palace. The King has been informed of your presence in the city and has expressed his wish to have you under his roof. The royal brigade did not exaggerate when they told us about you; you are truly the most extraordinary man ever to be seen in all the kingdoms of this world. You come, then, from?

– From up there.

– Where, up there?

– Up there where I was until today, before coming down into the light.

– Did you wait a long time before coming into the light?

– He must have waited nine months, just like everybody else.

– Thirty years or more, in fact most surely, thirty-two or thirty-three.

– Good grief!

– He's mocking us, you know, he's pulling our leg.

– He doesn't seem to be joking, keep quiet!

– Ask him when he was born.

– You ask him.

– When were you born?

– I don't know. I came down to the light this morning, at dawn.

– What the devil does he mean by this "came down"?

– He means that he was born this morning, that's what. To come and to be born, aren't they the same thing?

– But he says that he came *down*!

– What do we do when we're born, go *up*?

– But we don't descend either.

– Then he's a newly-born.

9

– Newly born so fully grown?

– But he's of smoke, he's of smoke; there's nothing to marvel at.

– Excuse me, were you born with your boots on?

– No, I found these as soon as I came down.

– And yet again with this coming down!

– He says "to come down" for "to be born," don't you understand yet, blockhead?

– Having lived thirty and more years, as you say, in your mother's womb, you must retain a vision, some memory of that time.

– Not a vision, but only the memory: I remember everything of every hour and every moment; it wasn't given me to see, around me all was black.

– Then you could see.

– Black.

– You could see black.

– But of course, of course, what's the point of making a long story of it, inside the womb black is all one can see. What did you see, blue?

– My dear fellow, in the womb you can't see a blessed thing!

– And he instead could see, and he saw black, that's what – a black uterus!

– A black uterus?

– Naturally, what's so odd about that?

– Just tell us, sir, how is it that you left your mother?

– When I came down those women were no longer there. And I came down precisely because I no longer heard their voices, and I burst into tears, weeping long, bitterly and desperately.

– Those women?…What women?

– *Pena! Rete! Lama!*

– And who are they?

– They are his mothers.

– But he's crazy!

– What what what?...

– Yes.

– You have three mothers?

– He's crazy!

– So, he has three mothers, what's so odd about that? When somebody is odd, he's odd in everything; it's quite understandable, what's so odd about that?

– *Pena! Rete! Lama! Pe...Re...La...*

– Let's call him Perelà!

– Let's call him Perelà!

– But no, Perelà, what does Perelà mean?

– There was a king whose name was Cuck. What does Cuck mean? So his name can be Perelà.

– But explain to us, clarify for us; for heaven's sake, what are we to tell the Sovereign?

– Where I stayed until this morning was not the womb of just any mother, but the top of a chimney.

– Ahaaaaah!

– Oooooh!

– Ho! Ho!

– That's it!

– Now I understand!

– A chimney!

– I understand it all!

– Poor devil!

– Some logs burned below me all the time; a low fire, and a coil of smoke rose all the way up the chimney to where I was. I don't remember when I acquired reason, the faculty of knowing and understanding. I began to exist, and gradually I became aware of my own being, I heard, I felt, I understood. In the beginning I heard an indistinct singsong, a confused murmur of voices that seemed one and the same to me, until finally I realized that below me there existed beings who had a close connection with my own being; I came to know myself and them, I learned to know others, I understood that that was life. Day by day I heard those voices better and better until I could make out words and their meaning to the point of seizing their most hidden nuances. Those words did not remain inert in me, they began the web of a mysterious and delicate work. Beneath me the fire burned uninterruptedly, and the warm coil came up and nourished every faculty of my being: I was a man. But I did not know how other men were, I thought they were all the same as I am.

– What a thought, poor man!

– Poor devil!

– It must have been a terrible moment!

– Around the fire three old women sitting in very large armchairs would take turns reading aloud or would talk to each other. From their lips I learned what all men learn first from their mothers and then from their teachers. *Pena, Rete, Lama* did not fail to prepare me and to apprise me of all useful knowledge concerning life, and they explained, exhaustively and insistingly, every idea and topic, every problem, every phenomenon. I learned of love and hate, of life and death, of war and peace, of work, of joy and grief, of wisdom and folly. With them I climbed the dizziest heights of thought and spirit...

– He must know a lot of things.

– What a cultivated man.

– Poetry and philosophy...

– Philosophy too?

– Yes, a light philosophy, extremely light, was what could come all the way up to me...

– Thank goodness.

– So light that it makes one rise to unattainable heights. And all things reached me in this way.

– So, what were the three old women called?

– *Pena, Rete, Lama.*

– What names!

– I knew a man whose name was Sandwich.

– What a novelty.

– But those were certainly not their real names, they were just conventional words that they used to identify themselves to one another. Oh! They must have been called otherwise, for sure. They had a reason for hiding from me their true names and their true nature, a reason I never discovered. Why did they want to hide everything from me? Why did they abandon me?

– But did those three old women know that you were up there at the top of the chimney?

– Did they know it? I never succeeded in finding out. They never said a word about me.

– And you never spoke up?

– Only this morning I realized I could talk, when I had no sooner come down...

– Not again!

– Go on!

– ...I called them for the first time: *Pena! Rete! Lama! Pena! Rete! Lama! Pe...Re...La...*

– Now he's starting to cry again.

– Don't cry anymore.

– Take heart, poor thing, or you'll make us cry, too.

– For heaven's sake, they were his mothers, let him cry as long as he wants!

13

– But if they were always there chatting and reading, they must have had a good reason.

– They could have been by the fireplace to keep warm.

– And they kept the fire lit in the summer too?

– Yes.

– Even in the month of August?

– Always.

– Old women are very sensitive to the cold, they no longer feel the heat.

– So then, they knew you were up there, and they were agreed not to speak of it. And what do you think about that?

– Was I amassed and created little by little by that warm coil that constantly came up? Cell by cell like the stones of a building? So that the product of that fire was used entirely for my construction...

– But didn't the smoke pass out of the chimney?

– The chimney was blocked at the top just where my head reached.

– Ah! That's it! The black uterus was sealed in the upper part.

– Just as all uteruses, it seems to me, up to now...

– Or, was I put up there one day, a man as I am now, but with flesh and clothes the same as those of all other men?

– That's it...they must have hidden you there!

– They put you there!

– Now we're getting somewhere!

– Those three old women must have had a secret.

– It's quite clear.

– As clear as day.

– A smoky secret!

– Who knows?

– That business of not wanting their names to be known...

– And of not wanting to talk about it with anyone.

– Not even with him!

– So then, from the effect of the fire, I must have carbonized slowly day by day, changing gradually over the years until I finally turned into the thickest possible smoke while still retaining my original shape – but I can't remember anything about that day or anything before it. Not until today could I realize that I am made of a substance that differs from that of all other men, while my shape is the same as theirs. Was this a thorough purification of the flesh accomplished by fire?

– Purification!

– Purification!

– Purification!

– Just so, quite so!

– Yes, yes, that's so!

– The purification of matter!

– He must have been a lover of those three old women, and to cleanse him of his sin, they...

– They must have been some bitches when they were young!

– Vulgar sluts!

– There must be something rotten behind this.

– Those nice old ladies had a lover.

– A lover! Are you kidding?

– How old were the old women?

– A hundred.

– Good Lord!

– And you, how long did you stay in that black uterus of yours?

– He told us, thirty or more years.

– And at seventy they had a lover?

– What's more...one same lover for the three of them.

– They were so old...

– Rest assured, Signor Perelà, that they hid you up there as a man, just as you are now. By virtue of being above the fire you turned into smoke, a most natural phenomenon. When we burn anything at all, we see that it first carbonizes and then turns into smoke.

– But smoke disperses in the air.

– That chimney was blocked at the top, therefore the smoke couldn't disperse in the air, that's only logical....Can you really think...amassed little by little...constructed...the germ of a man must have been at the top of that chimney, a uterus, black or white, always requires seed in order to produce anything.

– And the seed for a chimney is smoke.

– Everything fits perfectly.

– But not at all, not at all, since he's a man.

– Be quite assured, Signor Perelà, you were placed there in that chimney as you are, for the moment the reason escapes us, and you must indeed be thirty-two or thirty-three years old. What do you say to that?...

– I suppose so...

– I'd say he's older than that.

– He looks older than he is.

– He may look as old as you like, but he can't be that old.

– That's how long he's lived as a man...

– And he needed just as long to purify himself.

– In fact, thirty-three years of sin require thirty-three years of penance, it's been that way since the beginning of creation.

– Then he's sixty-six.

– Will you shut up, damn it all!

– You, Signor Perelà, are a man purified of all human dross. This will render you highly welcome in our eyes, an exceptional and privileged being – sublime.

– Imagine how pleased the King will be!

– The Queen will be wild with joy!

– Two of you hasten to His Majesty who waits anxiously, inform him that we have seen, touched, and interrogated the man, that he is among us, that he is truly of smoke, a perfect gentleman, and that there is nought to fear from him. Tell him to be at ease; we shall explain the matter to him in detail. Everything is much more readily understandable than might have seemed at first. Go quickly, make haste! So it is, Signor Perelà, it is our morbid imagination that causes us to think first of things that are complicated, impossible, absurd; simple things are the last to enter our mind.

– And so here we are. Splendid, truly splendid, worthy sir, we shall have your quarters made ready, and you have only to ask for whatever you may need.

– Certainly, most certainly, there can be no question about it, you were placed up there, for what reason we do not as yet know, but you will see without fail that we shall succeed in discovering it, your very clothes make that evident, we shall soon have the full and perfect revelation of your identity. My faith is absolute on this point. Be so kind as to turn around. Hmm...you're probably a Spaniard.

– Or a Frenchman?

– He's a Frenchman!

– If he were French, we'd know from his accent.

– He's an aristocrat who has fled from the Revolution. You can tell that from his clothes.

– But no, he's German, a gentleman of the Romantic cycle.

– He's an eighteenth-century Venetian.

– He's a Florentine of the Renaissance age.

– He's run away from the Revolution.

– Do those boots of his look to you as though they belong to the age of the Revolution?

– But he found them this morning, my dear chap, he found them before coming out of his hole up there.

– They don't have anything to do with him, they're not made of smoke.

– They're boots exactly like ours and made by a master shoemaker.

– Those old ladies had them made for him recently, they're identical to those of our officers.

– From their cut I'd say they're the work of my brother's shoemaker.

– Now, you see they knew what they were about. What would three old women do with a pair of boots?

– He's Dutch, no doubt about it.

– Not by a long shot, he's a baronet of the English court.

– You chaps still don't realize that he's a papal guard.

– As for me, he's a Turk.

– Signor Perelà, tell us the rest of your story, how did you decide to leave your hiding-place?

– It was three days ago that the sweet, familiar conversation ceased below me. I waited anxiously, but I no longer heard the adored voices that nourished my soul. Where had the old women gone? Their voices could no longer be heard. And shortly thereafter the fire also went out, the fire that had constantly nourished my body; around me everything became cold and silent, and I thought the hour of death had arrived for me. Instead my limbs gradually lost their immobility and began to stir, to move. I waited, feeling myself more and more invaded by a sense of desolation, of despair, of fright. *Pena, Rete, Lama,* where had they gone? Why had they left me alone? Had they abandoned me? Abandoned me forever? I began to stir and writhe in a spasm of anxiety, the straitness of the place had become unbearable once I lost my immobility, and I continued to writhe like a glob of foreign matter that had become virulent in an organ of the human body. I propped my hands against the walls, and by leaning with my back and forcing with my knees, I was able to descend to where the chimney gradually became wider and the links of the chain began. I grasped the chain and quickly came down to the ground. Below, the ashes were not yet cold, three empty arm-chairs stood about the fireplace, and on the floor was a large book that had been thrown down. It was closed. Next to where my feet had touched down was a pair of very beautiful, shiny boots – mine. I felt so strange on the ground where I stood unsteadily, and so drawn to rise that I had to force myself not to return up there despite myself. Instinctively I slipped my feet into the boots and only then did I feel steady, secure, firmly on earth and capable of staying on it. I let go of the chain, which I was still clutching so tightly, and I began to walk. I ran through all the rooms of the villa. Empty! Not a sign of life, not one person, not an animal, not a piece of furniture. I shouted until I felt that my throat would burst: *Pena! Rete! Lama!* No one! Nothing! I shrieked like a madman: *Pena! Rete! Lama!* I was in despair. It was as though a beast were devouring my heart, and just as I thought it was over with me, I found myself at the door of the villa. The door was open wide, before me lay the dusty road that leads to this city. Like a blind man I knew everything without ever having seen anything: the stories of all men, their deeds and their sentiments, without knowing exactly what they looked like; the names of all things without knowing the things to which those names corresponded, like a blind man who has received the gift of sight by enchantment. Now I was to see.

– The Royal Palace is surrounded by people, everybody wants to know, to see, to meet Perelà.

– Your name is known everywhere!

– Some claim to have seen him when he passed along the road, and they want to speak to him come what may.

– People are thronging at the gates!

– A huge crowd!

– And the guards are struggling to hold them back!

– The ladies of high society are telephoning from everywhere to acquire information.

– The King has ordered that Perelà be granted hospitality and accorded all the honors due a royal Prince.
– The Queen has announced that she will grant him a most private audience.
– The Court's Grand Master of Ceremonies of the Court is preparing the day's program.

– A number of important citizens request admission to your presence. May they be shown in?
– Signor Perelà, your name is on everyone's lips, they are speaking of nothing but you, the man of smoke, of your castle, of your mothers, of your boots...Perelà! Perelà! Perelà here, Perelà there.... It would take fifty men of smoke to satisfy so many people!

– Let signor Perelà pass into the reception hall; the majordomo will show in the first visitors.

– The great national sculptor, Cesare Augusto Bellezza.
– Most illustrious sir, I hold myself highly honored at being the first to be admitted into your presence, and without further delay I announce to you that it is my pondered resolve, as well as my duty, to provide our fatherland with your monument. In that bronze, which is sacred to the centuries and to heroes, your greatness and your likeness will be commemorated and immortalized.
– In bronze?
– Certainly, in bronze.
– Isn't bronze a very heavy matter?
– What do you mean by that? That with bronze one cannot express and reproduce the lightest

things? The flowing tresses of Venus newly
blossomed from the waves? The veils of all the
dancing maids of Hellas and Ninevah? The garru-
lous harmony emitted by the pipes of Narcissus'
lips while he admires himself in Nature's mirror
and Zephyr grazes his velvet cheek? But do you
know what bronze is?
– And do you know what smoke is?

– Her Majesty's painter, Gastone Speranza.
– Most excellent Signor Perelà, permit me to
pay my profoundest respects and to express my
deepest devotion. The honor that you lavish upon
me by having me meet a man, yes, I say...a man
such as you, is most highly appreciated by me. I am
sure that you will respond affirmatively to the
invitation I am about to make to you. I aspire to be
your first portraitist. You will be the model for my
masterpiece. No other portraitist will ever find so
inspiring a model as yourself, and at the next exhi-
bition you will be represented beside the Queen.
Allow me to submit to your infallible judgment
my latest work, the one that gained for me the post
I occupy. Moreover, a man of so high a rank cannot
fail to develop a major picture-gallery in his own
home, and I count on including your name as that of
my most illustrious client, after the name of our
Sovereign, of course. You there....Come forward....
Halt, stop. Unveil it. As you will observe, Signor
Perelà, she is a lady of the sixteenth century, the
century of grandeur and genius, and the cavalier
standing before her has just raised himself from a
kneeling position in which he had been declaring
his mad passion. The noble lady is sitting, do you
see? And with the index finger of her fair hand she

points to the Gothic window with its little mystical column. Do you see the deep-red rose that seems to have blossomed miraculously in an expectant night? Do you see it? Now then, with a noble gesture she says to him: "Take it." And is it not as though she were saying to him: "Your request is crowned by my love. Your long wait has ended, and you shall have that which is due a man. Here is the flower of which you were in need, it belongs to you, take it and preserve it in your breast as a pledge of the first kiss." Observe with what an eye she gazes upon him, and with what joy she indicates the scarlet rose on the sill of the mystical window. How many things a piece of canvas can say. The painting is appropriately called *Le Chevalier sans Rose.*

– What is that lady saying?

– Take it, the flower is yours.

– No, no.

– How, no?

– That's not what she says; rather she says: "Leave, sir."

– Oh, Signor Perelà, whatever are you saying? Do you not see how her eyes sparkle? And how her lips thirst for love and for kisses?

– Can't a lady smile while telling a man to leave?

– No, by no means; how could she say such a thing if she is pointing to the window?

– Can't one smile while leaving by a window?

– No, no, I assure you. It's as though she were to say to him "I'd like to see you break your neck." She cannot say that, absolutely not, what a thought, the meaning of the painting would be turned upside down. I implore you not to mention it to anyone;

you would thoroughly compromise this work of mine, which has secured me the post I occupy, and your erroneous interpretation would be fatal to me at this time....You there....Come forward....Halt, stop. Cover it up.

– Some photographers.

– Easy, easy, two at a time, there'll be time for all.

– Be so kind as to turn this way, sir.

– Meanwhile I'll use this opportunity to take a profile.

– Would you please be seated?

– And pretend to be reading the newspaper? Like this, with complete naturalness, as though you were sitting in a café. That's it, very good.

– And hold this cigarette between your fingers. In your other hand the match you have just taken from its box. Very good, an excellent pose: marvelous.

– Would you be so kind as to cross your legs like this?

– And your arms this way, placing your finger right here. Just so, perfect!

– Would you care to take off your boots?

– No!

– You could put them on again right away, of course, immediately.

– No!

– I myself would put them back on for you.

– No!

– It doesn't matter, don't bother, we'll do without that. It would have been wonderful for the movies, very effective.

– No!

– It doesn't matter, forgive me, please don't
bother, I do beg your pardon.

– Don't mention it.

– Please.

– That's it.

– Thank you.

– Best wishes.

– My respects.

– Much obliged.

– Most excellent sir.

– Most illustrious sir.

– Very much obliged.

– Vruchbliged...

– The State's banker, Teodoro Di Sostegno.

– As soon as I learned of your presence in our
city, I hastened to pay my respects and at the same
time to beg you to listen to what in a few words I
am about to tell you. I heard also that you have
arrived without much of anything and in possession
only of a pair of boots.

– These.

– One can hardly speak of your financial status
as impressive; therefore I come to offer you unlimited credit at my bank: I am placing my money at
your disposal. And this, of course, not to benefit
you alone, but so that as partners we may conduct
some excellent business.

– Me?

– You, to be sure.

– But I am made of smoke.

– That is precisely why.

– And how can I, of so humble a nature, be the
source of riches?

– My friend, you are of smoke, and I, in the final analysis, am of paper, every action of mine is carried out and completed by means of paper, take note, it doesn't even have to be clean, often it's in terrible condition, disgusting, now I can demonstrate to you as easily as two and two make four that between paper and smoke the distance is quite small, minimal. Not only that, but smoke being nothing but the sublimation of paper, it works a hundred thousand times more effectively. Leave it to me, no one can outdo me in this business. You are of smoke, I know what smoke is. And as soon as I heard that it was available in its natural state, I immediately said to myself: there's not a minute to lose. And I hurried to you here. Everything can become hard cash in our pocket, and smoke to an unlimited degree. The sun, for example, which appears to be something inaccessible, unreachable, is nothing but a big bank note that, if you manage to cash it, you can spend at your heart's content. And that's to say nothing of the moon.

– The sun?

– The sun itself.

– That's true, because if it were a metal coin, it would be too heavy and would fall.

– It would have fallen who knows how long ago, that's an inescapable fact; instead, being a piece of paper, extremely light, it stays up all the time, like a kite.

– And you cash it?

– That's all we do from morning to night. Here's my address, you can phone me whenever you like. I've briefly laid the groundwork for a new company of which you shall be the president, I the managing director: the S.O.H. *smoke only hope.* You will see just how far we can go with this incredibly refined substance.

– Perhaps where not even you imagine.

– I am at your service for whatever you may need. We're agreed, then, Signor Perelà, my compliments.

– The poet, Angiolino Dal Soffio.

– When I heard your name spoken in the street, I was strolling with my mistress who is blonde like Venus and like Isolde. The name, which on the uncouth lips of the common herd had left me indifferent, acquired upon hers its true significance. I made her repeat your name over and over, just as every evening before putting out the light I have her repeat over and over the eternal word. What analogies, what correspondences. On her lips *Pe...re...là...* can be seen to take flight swiftly and airily, as one sees depart to rise lightly, delicately, another word: *po...ë...sy....* Do you feel all the fascination of this bewitching word? Ah, what a *p* is like on those lips, Signor Perelà, like the quivering force that quickens and gives life. Who will assist me in telling you what the *s* is like, the *s* that sustains that word from below and lifts it, and drives it, driving, driving, on high...higher...ever higher....Poetry, Signor Perelà, is a world, a globe all of gold, of gold alone, of the kind that is not coined, and it is the poet, on Parnassus, who inflates it, with his divine breath, preparing it for its celestial ascent. What is the secret? It is to know how to inflate it, to the very point of making it transparent, so that it may rise lightly and swiftly, to the point of making it glow, so that all the world may admire it, so that all the world may behold it.

   – And do you go up with it?

   – A foreign body? Oh, dear me! If I were to hold on to it, that would be the end, there's no way it could rise, it would remain on earth forever. When I have properly inflated it I send it aloft. I remain on Parnassus.

   – I imagine you must take care when you inflate the globe so that nothing gets into it.

   – No doubt about it, the slightest bit of the simplest substance would keep it from rising. It looks as if something extraordinary is inside this dazzling globe, and instead there isn't anything. To attain emptiness is the sublime art of the poet. What simplicity, and what complexity: this is lightness! In your honor I shall compose a hymn of thirteen thousand hendecasyllables and one dactylic septenarius. I'll send it to you when it's published in the nation's leading journal. In the meantime I have for you my latest book of verses: *Ballate... malate (Ailing...Ballads)*.

   – What a pity, poor things.

   – Don't grieve for them.

   – What are they suffering from?

   – They are perfectly fine.

   – Then why do you say they are ailing?

   – Otherwise, nobody would care about their well-being. Even so people pay little attention to them. If they saw all of them croak together they wouldn't give up a sigh for them, we live in a materialistic age, without poetry and without heart. Count on my friendship as I hope to count on yours. After all, both of us are poets, and we could co-author a poem. We will write it, I have every confidence. Following me, Signor Perelà, will come the critic, Cristoforo Soffiato, born to drive me mad. I entreat you not to believe a single word he says, he's out there waiting, watching for me to leave so that he can come in, he always comes after me, it's his inferiority, but he's always at my heels, it's my damnation. Without doubt he will speak to you about me. And what could he speak to you about, the backbiter, the poltroon: *Monsieur de Perelà, j'espère bien tôt de vous rencontrer dans le monde.*

– Cristoforo Soffiato, critic of the nation's official literature.

– Don't be surprised if I come to you after that wretch. Fate willed that I give precedence to him, but that won't be the case much longer, and you will soon see things go the other way.

– Who, the man with the balloon?

– In person. He could very well put off his singing until I've had my say, don't you think? We already know beforehand what he'll say, from the first word to the last.

– And does he make you see it inflated or yet to be inflated?

– What?

– The balloon.

– He makes me see it inflated.

– And must you go up there to where he sends it?

– What?

– The balloon.

– No, fancy that. It's he who goes, I don't budge an inch, I have a telescope. Are you familiar with the critic's telescope? It's the longest of all, but it's the most collapsible. I carry it in my vest pocket: look!

– The great philosopher of pessimism. Guscio Cima, called Cimone del Guscio.
– I'm not a philosopher at all, you know. Never pay attention to what they say. When a man has said the worst about his own species, they say he's a philosopher – what they mean by the word isn't clear – and the more he flails them, the greater a philosopher he's proclaimed. Man needs to speak ill of his fellow-men, it is no less vital a need than air and bread, and having neither the courage nor the imagination to succeed at it, he finds the truths spoken by someone else and ends by thinking that he himself has discovered them. In this way each one sees his fellow-man submerged in the mire, and stands there looking at him as though he himself wasn't in it up to his neck. But tell me something: how did you happen to land here? What's your purpose in coming here?
– Nothing.
– Well then, do yourself a favor without delay: go back to where you were until now, you'll be better off; you'll get to know human beings some other time, and you won't have missed anything. I really wouldn't want you to meet them just now. Do you too aspire to become a gnawing worm like all the others? Humans gnaw away nature's dwellings exactly as termites gnaw away human dwellings. And do you know what reason they adduce to justify such gnawing? They say that the earth attracts them. Yes, indeed, they are attracted to it. They have taken root in it and continue to reproduce with the rapidity of insects. The earth

would like nothing better than to be rid of them, by throwing them off, all of them, they are her most indigestible dish, they stick in her throat and sicken her, she hasn't been able to stomach a single one of them. Once in a while she gives a big jolt and squashes a few of them, then pretends to be unaware of them and lets them alone until, remembering them again, she gives another big jolt: *crack!* However, there is one thing that humans have created and continue to create on earth, and you have to give them credit for it: dust. Look where they walk, endlessly dragging their vanities, observe the roads they have travelled, trailing all kinds of vehicles that might get the ground to yield as much dust as it can. They use boulders to manufacture objects that fit in the palm of one's hand. Today you see a rocky mountain that seems inaccessible. Well, if humans start to stroke it, prod it, scratch it, riddle it, in a short while you'll see it no more because they will have turned it into so many saltcellars. Take a good tree, large, sturdy, straight, majestically occupying its own place on the earth, its rightful realm. They begin to move around it; they get at its roots, and by filing, scraping, boring, they get it to fall, but there's no chance of their causing it to come down on their heads; at just the right moment they scurry out of the way, and then it falls. You feel its crash in your heart, and before you know it, you discover that they're busy picking their teeth with that tree. Listen to me, go back home. Don't let yourself be enticed by smiles and caresses, by flattery – don't go for any of it if you want to survive. They enjoy raising a man on high only to double their pleasure in letting him fall. The higher they raise him, the more enjoyable the crash.

– But I'm made of smoke.

– Ah, quite so. I had forgotten. Then do stay, my worthy friend: *ciao!*

– The Court-physician, Sebastiano Pipper.

– I am the Court-physician, Signor Perelà, physician of the gentlemen and of the lovely ladies. Do you know what a physician is? A physician is a whole row of the most complicated and absurd things, and I am lost day and night trying to understand the make-up of this disquieting human body that looks as though it were the most perfect mechanism and instead is a gross, shocking, shameful abnormality. Indeed, it is of an impudence and vulgarity that severely try the stomach of one who exercises my profession.

– If you but knew how carefully a man of science must watch his tongue. He may joke with that of others, but he must beware of his own. The whole secret lies in this: in saying...and in not saying. Your pronouncements are always good and in your favor; the facts are what screw you. For instance, if you say: "the patient will recover," the bastard croaks in less than an hour. And if instead you say: "he's sure to die," within two days of having received the last sacrament he recovers and is up and about. Sickness and medicine form the most capricious match known. For thousands of years they've done nothing but spite one another, tell lies to one another, lay traps and snares for one another – woe if one falls for their cajoling ways! – only for this pleasure do they live together. How is your pulse?...Good...normal. Your tongue?...Excellent.

Your color is fine. Here's my card, for whenever my services may be of use to you. Signor Perelà, I am at your beck and call.

   – His Eminence, the Most Reverend Cardinal Archbishop.
   – And so, you are called?...
   – Perelà.
   – Just so. Very good. Pe...relà; splendid! Perelà. My dear Signor Perelà, I am quite sure I can number you among the chosen sheep of my beloved flock, since you are after all but a man.
   – A very light one.
   – Oh! Come, come, come, my dear man! To be light in one's body matters not at all. You, more than anyone else, are in need of assistance and protection. It is one's soul that must be light, and the soul acquires lightness only with the daily practice of virtue and the forswearing of one's errors, one's sins. Only then can it rise to Heaven. It is an act of humility by which even kings, indeed they above all, have felt themselves elevated and exalted.
   – What is the soul made of?
   – The soul is pure spirit.
   – Can it be seen?
   – But no, spirit can't be seen, it is revealed beyond and above our senses.
   – Then you have never seen a man rise to Heaven?
   – The souls of all the elect rise without our being able to observe it.
   – And the others?
   – The others plunge into the depths of Hell most foul.
   – Because they are too heavy.

– Precisely. They were not freed from the weight of their sins.

– Indeed. Indeed.

– Gentlemen, may we have a little calm and a little silence? The Grand Master of Ceremonies is about to read the Program. Silence!

– The Program:

Tomorrow, Friday, at five o'clock sharp, the ladies of High Society and of the Court will hold a tea in honor of Signor Perelà.

– With the participation of the Queen?

– No. Silence!

No other men will be invited along with him. His Majesty the King has given special orders so that the party may be of a particular intimacy, as intimate as possible, the King says, and formal at the same time.

The day after tomorrow, Saturday, at five o'clock sharp, Her Majesty the Queen will receive Signor Perelà in a most private audience.

Sunday evening at nine o'clock, Signor Perelà will be presented to the people. Accompanied in the Royal Carriages by a retinue of the principal gentlemen and ladies of the Court and High Society, he will tour the capital's main streets and its suburbs. On the municipal knoll the Mayor, who will be awaiting him there, will offer him the greetings of the entire citizenry.

The city will be illuminated, hung with flags, and festively decorated: large candles, Chinese lanterns, fireworks and Bengal lights, crackers, and thundering salvos everywhere, and in the squares no less than fourteen bands will play. The same evening at eleven o'clock, a Court Ball which our Sovereign will attend.

   – Long live the King!

   – Viva!

   – In addition...silence, I said! In addition, His Majesty the King appoints Signor Perelà as the third member of the Committee for the weighty, difficult and long overdue compilation of the new Code for our country.

   – Long live the King!

   – Viva!

   – Long live the new Code!

   – Viva!

   – Long live the Code of Perelà!

The Tea

– We are all so very flattered, aren't we, my dears?
– Indeed!
– Very much so!
– All of us!
– *Very* much!
– Infinitely.
– Really!
– Yes!
– Truly!
– Rather!
– Signor Perelà, we are so very flattered to meet...
– Such a man as you!
– The King has commanded us to receive you with the greatest honor.
– With the maximum honor.
– And in the closest intimacy.
– Such as has not been granted anyone in Court for a very long time.
– The King!
– You shall be the glory of his Reign.
– Very likely the sole glory.
– And he has made known to us that whatever your request may be, we are not to say "No" to you.
– You could have kept that to yourself, it's strictly confidential.
– You made a mistake in telling him. One never knows...
– But you will be discreet, won't you?
– We have your promise.

36

– All too discreet, don't be alarmed.

– He will be as he chooses to be.

– From this moment we count on your delicacy.

– And on your sense of honor.

– How can we arouse his interest?

– If we bore you, you need only say "Enough."

– And we shall be silent.

– You will have obtained the most that can be gotten from a woman.

– Something that no man has ever succeeded in getting.

– We are here to obey you, isn't that so, darlings?

– Absolutely!

– Certainly!

– Rather!

– Yes, to be sure.

– Indeed, indeed.

– Yes, yes!

– How can we prove our devotion to you? Our affection?

– We know everything about you; you should know something about us, if it doesn't displease you.

– But is it true, Signor Perelà, that you will prescribe the new Code for our country?

– Of course, didn't you hear them last night?

– They didn't say he would prescribe it; they said he would assist the Minister and Torlindao in compiling it.

– Third member.

– No, my dear, they said he would *prescribe* it, *prescribe* it, *prescribe* it.

– Third member!

– Good heavens, so he's to prescribe it! In any case, what do I care?

– You're saying that he's not to prescribe it, but he is.

– Third member.

– Darlings, it's an idle question; we shall see whether or not he is to prescribe it. Do be quiet. Our present laws, Signor Perelà, are in need of drastic changes. As for this blessed Code which is always in the making but never gets done, we're at least a hundred years behind the times. Little is said of women in the old Code, and that little is always to their disadvantage or beside the point. Women must have a part in many more matters, in all matters if things are to go as they should. These men understand next to nothing.

– Nothing at all.

– And they pretend to know everything.

– In order to boss us around.

– That's the trouble.

– And the old Code is made expressly for that.

– A relic that should be thrown into the fire!

– With it they are always in the right.

– Do you want a cup of tea?

– Tea.

– Here comes the tea.

– Signor Perelà...

– Do have some.

– Will you?

– Help yourself.

– May I?

– Look at how he drinks it!

– He takes a little sip from each of us.

– Two drops.

– No, he hardly rests his lips on the edge of the cup.

– What a dear!

– What a gentle soul.

– What a darling!

– Ah!

– From me, too, won't you?

– And nothing at all from me? Ah, I knew you would.

– I'll drink later from his cup.

– And you, why have you kept behind?

– Signor Perelà, don't take tea from her.

– What has she done to it, may we know?

– She was giving it to him without sugar – unsweetened.

– Wicked thing!

– Spiteful!

– Mean and unobliging!

– Spitefulspitefulspiteful!

– Do you like it?

– Really and truly?

– Ooh!

– He even takes tea!

– What a dear.

– But then, you're a man like all the others.

– Much much better than the others.

– I would never have believed that I'd meet a man of smoke.

– And offer him tea.

– And that he would drink it!

– It seems like a dream to me.

– And yesterday when they announced that you were in town I refused to believe it. More of their nonsense, I thought, they come up with something new every day.

– I was one of the last to believe it; but now...
here you are.

– I've always loved smoke, so it didn't surprise
me a bit.

– And I've always been wild about smoke, too.
You know, in July when I'm staying at my mother-
in-law's, from the window of her villa I can see the
big smokestack of a factory. I've passed whole
hours following the flight of the smoke. At times it
comes out breathed by the lips of the smokestack as
if it were speaking with somebody far far away and
making an effort to be understood: *hah*!... *pha*!...
plah...plah plah!...At other times instead, it's all
straight and black, or very low, as though chasing
after someone to do something to him; it seems as
if it has a stick in its hand. Another time I saw a
long trail of young girls come out holding each
other by the hand, you remember the paperdolls we
made out of newspaper when we were children?

– The brides of Perelà.

– And so when they told me that a man of smoke
had come to our town, I wasn't at all taken aback.
And right away I said: "Oh? but I've seen a hundred
thousand of them from my mother-in-law's window,
in the month of July." Signor Perelà, is it all right
if I caress you a little bit here, on the arm? Feel,
feel, my dears, it's so soft it will make you swoon.
Feel.

– Ooh!

– Incredible.

– It can't be true!

– Thrilling!

– My God!

– Ooh!

– How soft!

– How delicate!

– Just feel, feel.

– Feel him here.

– Are you like this all over?

– A cat.

– Much softer.

– A swan.

– Much softer.

– Like down.

– A hundred times softer.

– A gentle cloud.

– That's it!

– Or one of those large plumes that shoot out of locomotives.

– How wonderful!

– Feel him here.

– Where?

– In this spot.

– Oh, you hussy!

– Before burning, Signor Perelà, your suit must have been of a magnificent velvet.

– Ruby red! Blazing!

– Be quiet, silly goose.

– And now like this, all gray...

– A sinister plumage.

– Why sinister, my dear? He looks so honest.

– And good.

– And kind, don't you see how he lets himself be caressed?

– I only meant to say mysterious.

– Tonight, thinking of you, I won't be able to fall asleep. Tell me, Signor Perelà, tell me that you too won't sleep tonight.

– Please don't answer her! You see, our dear friend the Marchesa di Bellonda is a sweet and mild creature, but she has such a romantic and impressionable nature, and if you encourage her you will fall victim to her fantasies.

– Instead let's begin a tale.

– But a light tale...

– Extremely light...

– Of the kind he likes.

– Will we succeed in winning your interest?

– In amusing you?

– If we bore you say so quickly and we won't say another word.

– Do you need anything?

– Would you care for more tea?

– A sandwich?

– A fondant?

– A sugarplum?

– A cookie?

– Yesterday our gentlemen very likely kept you amused with their varied topics, but we...poor women, we have so few we can draw upon...

– For a man like him.

– What do you mean?

– I know what I mean.

– Be quiet, silly! What do you know about him?

– Each one of us is to search the depths of her heart for the lightest thing there...

– Something that will suit you.

– And if you hear the same thing from all of us, do pardon us, we are so shut off. Our gentlemen can place themselves on a pedestal with their vaunted intelligence...

– Which they don't have.

– With their cunning and bullying.

– You can say that again.

– With their knowledge and money...

– When they have a lot of it.

– As for us, only beauty can win us any privileges. Politics admits not a single brushstroke of our color on its canvas.

– Religion admits us only as an ornamental frame, we are listeners and no more, extras.

– You will agree that listening is a rather hard lot.

– Always listening, only listening.

– Ugh! What a bore.

– We can't celebrate Mass.

– Science puts no trust in us, and art...if it be not that of song....Men allow us only to treasure and profit from that bit of love which they demand of us for their own amusement in their spare time or, worse yet, as a brutal need for their disgusting bodies.

– Zoë will be first to speak. She deserves precedence. As you can observe, Signor Perelà, she surpasses all of us by far in beauty, she's considered the most beautiful woman in our kingdom. Come Zoë, begin your tale.

The Duchess Zoë Bolo Filzo

– All the men of fashionable society have lost their heads over her.

– And she has held them up to ridicule, from first to last.

– She has laughed at all of them.

– And she hasn't yielded to any of them.

– There are those who say she hasn't yielded even to her husband.

– She's of such iciness as to be frightening.

– Four or five have killed themselves because of her.

– Five? At least a dozen.

– She made a seventy-year-old baron die of a broken heart!

– A millionaire.

– A bachelor.

– With loads of nephews.

– One of those men, Signor Perelà, from whom not even our venerated Saviour is able to liberate us.

– She's brought as much profit to the railroads as have the crowds of pilgrims who go to Rome.

– A young marquis promised her that he would kill himself after just one kiss of hers. She refused to grant him the kiss, and he...he killed himself just the same.

– He must have been a great fool.

– Really, darling, that time you were diabolically wicked.

– She lures them into her web only to let them pine.

– Not allowing a man willing to die for us to die with our kiss upon his lips.

– Ah, you are sick with romantic nonsense. After my kiss the dear marquis, in hopes of obtaining the rest, would no longer have killed himself, or he would have gone about joking that the kisses of the most beautiful of women have after all the same taste as those of any other woman. You see, Signor Perelà, in their readiness to yield to this man and that, these good friends of mine do not give themselves a moment to think of a strategy, and so they end up humiliated, disillusioned, disgusted, victims of the vagaries and the brutality of men. Instead

men should be made to reckon with our virtue.
Don't they want us to be virtuous, pure, chaste?

– Yes, in word.

– Let us be so unconditionally and we will make
them happy.

– You know better than we do what they want.

– They live their lives in the most varied fields
of action, where they can freely develop or exercise
every sort of energy, every faculty. As for us...they
have penned us in a single field. Well then, let us
wait for them there. Why force their gates? Let us
ready ourselves for the time when they come knock-
ing at ours. And let us employ all our resources to
that end. What does it matter to me if the men who
approach me are experts in politics or in science,
skillful in art or in industry? They are at a total loss
in my science, in my art, in my industry. They do not
know that for every action of mine a corresponding
counteraction is available to them, one capable of
neutralizing my action: in fact they drink it up with
eyes shut, the way a drunkard empties one glass
after another; they drink us up, they gulp us down,
and when they are satiated, filled with us, they
burst. And, I say, let them burst. I am simply
thrilled when I see them around me so tipsy; in a
grotesque way, they brighten this monotonous and
gray existence of ours. When I was a child, at night
in the garden of a kind grandfather of mine I would
have the servants look for as many toads as could
be found, and on the back of each one I would pour
a good amount of gasoline or kerosene, and then
with a match I would set them on fire, leaving them
free to run and jump. The poor little creatures
would jump while burning, and all those little
flames could be seen in the darkness of the garden.

The closer the flame got to their flesh, the more
their jumps became acrobatic, amazing, fantastic. I
laughed...laughed....Signor Perelà, how I laughed
at such a spectacle. My kind grandfather died, and I
went no more to his villa; but so many obliging
men have been good enough to continue the spectacle of those toads for me outside that garden.
And now watch me closely. I lay my hand just so,
with languid nonchalance, on my left hip – say we
are at a ball or at a tea. Behind me I've noticed a
gentleman whom I don't know and who for the last
few minutes has been following me as though
drawn by a magnet; he fixes his gaze upon me; he
stares at me without blinking. Little by little his
eyes begin to bulge. You could swear that in a few
minutes they will pop out of their sockets. I go on
speaking ever so casually with my dear friend. I
take my hand from my hip, and with both hands I
lean forward against the back of a very low chair,
crossing my legs like this, carefree, as though I
were certain of not being observed by a living soul.
My dress, which is probably of very shiny satin or
of very soft velvet, tightens around me, seconding
my every movement, like the skin of a dolphin. But
even more tenaciously than my dress, that fine
gentleman behind me clings to me with his gaze.
Take a look at him, just as I do, quickly and with
complete unconcern, as though he were a piece of
furniture in the drawing-room. He has already taken
on the air of the most perfect idiot to be seen, an
air so natural and so unfeigned: glistening eyes,
clenched teeth, lips slightly apart, and nostrils
open wide as though smelling avidly. And he becomes redder and redder, like a lobster boiling in a
pot. At this point he draws an elegant handkerchief

from his breast-pocket and brings it to his forehead: he's perspiring. All of a sudden I straighten up, and with both hands I start to gather up a few locks that I can feel falling down the back of my neck: there, like this! The gentleman can't control himself. Ever so quickly I skim my eyes over him and hasten to fix them at the other end of the room where without doubt there is a very dear friend of mine to whom I signal with a broad smile, giving my lips a particular rippling because of my unrestrainable joy in seeing her again and my unrestrainable desire to give her a kiss, she's so good, she's such a dear, and I do give her the kiss, I throw it to her, I send it to her on my fingertips, all the more affectionate for the distance that separates us. That man will get himself introduced to me, he'll besiege my house, manage to gain entrance, smother me with flowers and passionate notes, declare his mad love in a hundred ways, go to the brink of the usual suicide or only threaten it and end up with a little trip to the seashore or the mountains in search of some fresh air.

– How can a man be such a fool?

– I don't betray my husband – good heavens, no – I'm an honorable woman, virtuous.

– It sounds like a fable and yet it's true. She always succeeds amazingly well in this little game.

– I do not betray my husband. Are not men the ones who devised the law? Why break it? I find it stupendous, perfect. We are here to observe it in the strictest fashion.

The Princess Nadia Giunchi del Bacchetto

– Worthy sir, and you, my poor friends: I absolutely refuse not only to say anything at all about my life, but even to address any word or to proffer my hand to this crèche that you have so carefully taken in and that you now treat with such devotion. I am disgusted by his presence and even more by your stupid behavior.

– Well!

– You are committing a terrible offense to him and to all of us!

– And you are going against an order of the King!

– Every citizen, beginning with the King, has resolved to offer proper hospitality to this extraordinary figure.

– Beginning with the King!

– So much the worse for her, she'll lose favor with the Court.

– Without doubt.

– She's already at odds with the Court.

– And in a bad light.

– You are the only one who talks in such a way. Nobody else among us refuses to confide in Signor Perelà.

– He is to prescribe the new Code!

– Third member.

– You're in for it, my little one!

– Fools! Senseless creatures! This fellow boldly claims to be of smoke, isn't that so?

– He is.

– Have you gone blind?

– Don't you have eyes to see him?

– Didn't you pat him just now?

– Did you feel how soft he is?

– He dissolves at the touch.

– Of smoke. Can one imagine anything more loathsome, more irritating, more repellent?

– It's such a beautiful thing!

– Perhaps the only one.

– May he get into your nostrils, your eyes and your throats and so become intolerably odious to you.

– Be quiet!

– Silly goose!

– He won't get into anything at all!

– Signor Perelà is not the sort of man to do certain things.

– Unfortunately.

– He's extremely well-bred, more so than somebody I know.

– He's the most exquisite man I know.

– So melancholy in his exceptional nature!

– I say only this to you: do not pose one question to me, and go right on revealing your stupid secrets. Remember, however, that not only will that charming fellow laugh at you and your ridiculous tales, but that I shall be the first to do so.

– How uncouth!

– We'll see that the King hears of this.

– You'll be expelled from Court.

– And in disgrace.

– You won't set foot there again.

– Is it true, Signor Perelà, that you will laugh at us?

– You won't, will you?

– How could it be?

– Utterly impossible.

– Forgive this little incident, Signor Perelà, don't give it any thought, it's of no consequence, that rash woman doesn't know what she's saying.

– But forgiveness is all his joy. Is he not made for the sublime sweetness of giving?

Aldo Palazzeschi

– My dear Oliva, each day you too become more
unbearable with your melancholy. What's happening
to you to cause you to suffer so? You are tormented,
my little one, that's obvious. Pay no heed to her,
Signor Perelà, she has such a gloomy disposition
that she often makes the rest of us gloomy as well.
– It's a contagious disease.
– And she makes us pass some awful days. Lady
Gioconda,would you care to say something?

Lady Maria Gioconda Di Cartella

– Among all these ladies, gentle friend, I am
precisely the one who for the sake of discretion
should remain silent. My life has been nothing but
seclusion, resignation, and prayer. Twenty-five
years ago I became the bride of Signor Di Cartella,
but he failed to overcome my maidenhood. He did
not succeed that day, nor has he succeeded since. I
am still the pure maid of sixteen that I was when
delivered into my mother's arms by the beloved
Mother Superior of the convent where I was
trained. Young, naïve, passionate, disillusioned,
hurt, I was on the verge of plotting revenge by
seeking elsewhere that natural solace for my
exuberant youth – solace which was denied to me in
my legitimate union. Then...I chose to forget, and I
summoned all my strength to win a battle over
myself: and win it I did. A very sad thing, but I am
contented. My good companion, who could not
have from me the enthusiasm and devotion of love,
received the most faithful and affectionate compan-
ionship that a sister could bestow here on earth.
– A legendary generosity.
– It would have been such a simple thing...

– To find somebody who could make up for what was missing.

– And if need be...to make a change.

– Again?

– Could it be that the men who came her way were all like that?

– One never knows, when a thing gets off to a bad start.

– My good friends, life consists also of patience.

– Yes, but sometimes it runs out.

– Mine would have run out a long time ago.

– You know that as a dowry I brought to Signor Di Cartella all my mother's debts, and that even now my mother has not stopped writing him letters full of bitter reproaches, and even insults, because of his involuntary misfortune, and for the sole purpose of extracting money from him. I gave myself over to women's pursuits, and now I am the president of many charitable institutions for girls in danger of falling and for those who have been abandoned.

– She, who is so safe from danger!

– And I founded the Society for the Emancipation of Women. My days go by filled with work and interest; and so my life has not been an unhappy one. However, there is something, Signor Perelà, something that bothers me a lot and causes me anguish. Signor Di Cartella, once in a while...as though at fixed intervals...two or three times a year with the change of seasons...feels like attempting once again the arduous task: an illusion like any other. Twenty-five years have gone by, and I know in the minutest detail exactly what will happen, yet I must humor him. He believes...he deludes himself again...trying to find a new impetus or experiment-

ing a new method...thinking he has finally discovered the right way...again he deludes himself...
- Sure...just wait.
- I'd say to him: darling, by now I know, enough!
- He becomes agitated...flustered...he suffers... and drops back into even greater weariness.
- It was clear from the start.
- Signor Perelà, what anguish...what anguish!

The Countess Carmen Ilario Denza

- I had, Signor Perelà, a very precocious adolescence. From the time I was twelve I acquired a rather conspicuous masculine look, and my body took on a manly aspect throughout. There's nothing in me of that gracefulness and apparent softness that envelops my dear companions. When at sixteen I left the convent to enter into society, I already felt within me – though, without any understanding of such matters – the urgent need to be near a man. Fortune was always against me. Though this terrible anguish grew within me, I was unable to find a young man who showed interest in me. On the horizon I saw no promise, no hope of ending my torment. I could not conquer this fever of mine, I suffered, I passed whole nights writhing on the floor, I struggled to suppress my urge, I stifled my spasms, I castigated my rebellious flesh, I was hurting myself...but it was useless, useless, useless. My cheeks turned a horrible flushed color, like those of big country bumpkins, and certain wine-red blotches blossomed in the center of them. This made men take even less interest in me, I did not exist for them, just as though I were not a woman. I was pure and innocent and wanted to keep myself so, but my veins could not restrain the blood that coursed through them like a liquid flame, to become dynamite that exploded horribly in my heart, reducing my wretched strength to a murky pool. Perhaps, I thought to myself, I had passed more than a hundred times along the street where lived the man who, had he seen me, might have become interested in me. I should have passed five minutes sooner or five minutes later. Perhaps more than once we walked in the same direction, parallel to one another, and thus we could not meet.

During those years three close members of my family died, and dressed all in mourning I looked like a large widow – something that definitively removed men's interest in me.

By then I was twenty-five years old and the first man had not yet approached me, whereas I would have accepted the last of men. My sensibility had become so acute that, like a beast, I could detect along the street the acrid odor of a male, and like a beast I would follow these wilds scents that made me, once in my room, fantasize and rave, pushing me to the edge of madness.

One night I fled, reckless, lowering myself from the window down to the garden. I went out determined to lie with the first man I should meet. I ran through the deserted streets. I was at the barracks where thousands of men were immersed in their youthful sleep, and I was about to shout so as to wake all of them together: "Hey! What about it? Get up for a change!" Any one of them, perhaps, awakening in my arms, would have been happy. And meanwhile I had lost control of myself and might have lost myself forever. Worn-out, distraught, crushed, I recovered something of my reason and was seized with cold and fear. I rushed home thinking that the next day I could find somebody, that I would make a servant come up to my room; but to be discovered there, in that way and at that hour would have been an unbearable shame. Through the garden window I regained my room.

Two weeks later a friend came to visit my father; he had been sent by Count Ilario Denza. We had never seen each other; we met, and in less than three months our marriage of pure convenience was celebrated.

Count Ilario Denza came at me with the same eagerness, I believe, as any other normal and healthy man in his position. I do not blame him in the least, but I...what I had to suffer and at what cost of anguish and mortification I managed to remain passive and let him have his way with me. Because of my rage at not being able to repulse him, I felt the claws of madness pierce my brain and tear it to pieces, depriving it of all cohesion, all vital wholeness, all sense. Then the void before me, as though the most brutal violence had been done to my body. A being other than myself rebelled desperately within my person, outraged by the offense. The following morning I fled to my father and told him that if the Count were to repeat his act I would either kill myself or would kill him on the spot. Our separation was arranged that very day. Ten years of excruciating expectation that ended in a cry of disgust and pain at the touch of reality. Signor Perelà, without knowing it I was carrying within me a man, my true husband, who would admit neither violation nor betrayal.

– At least she is sure that they will be compatible with one another for life, isn't that so, Signor Perelà?

The Countess Chloe Pizzardini Ba

– My dear Signor Perelà, if you have not been struck by the tales of my good friends, you will be struck by mine because of its very naturalness. Tell me frankly, don't you find them a bit exaggerated and terribly complex, often downright extravagant? I consider this natural phenomenon as one of life's daily necessities. I cannot grant it any glamor beyond this, nor any aura of mystery, and it's no more important than my breakfast, my lunch or my dinner. I should inform you, however, that I eat heartily three times a day and believe that one must never say no the first time. I will add that I do not have any special memories or nostalgia, and that if any pleasant impressions have remained in my mind, they are connected not with the aristocratic and cultivated classes, but rather with the lower classes in whom there is no artifice whatever, but only spontaneity.

– Signor Perelà, go right ahead! Chloe has never sent anybody away with a no.

– At least not the first time.

– You wouldn't give a negative response this time, would you?

– By no means, my dear. I merely allow myself to express certain reservations in the matter. Forgive my frankness, Signor Perelà, but it seems to me that smoke...good heavens...I have always preferred the roast.

Aldo Palazzeschi

The Marchesa Oliva di Bellonda

– You see before you the woman who has never loved; the woman who could not love. Do you know that each of us, when born, bears within his breast someone else's heart? A maiden the heart of a youth, and the youth that of a maiden? We search throughout the world for our heart just as the beggar seeks his piece of bread. Wandering thus while bearing a heart whose rightful owner we seek, we may at a certain moment believe that we have found him: but all appearances deceive us, all hopes betray us. When we finally put our hearts one upon the other, we realize, too late, that the one we have found is not ours and that we do not have that of our companion. I have not found my heart and it is to no avail that I guard that of the man I shall never find. I am indissolubly bound to the man who did not have mine and to whom I could not give his own which I did not have. I have wandered to the point of utter exhaustion in search of him. Where is he? Is he dead? Where is he hidden? Who conceals him from me? Does he belong to another woman? Is his fate like mine? Who has stolen him from me? Henceforth I am disconsolate, and even now I see myself roving from door to door with my burden of love. Perhaps he too searches in pain as I do. Why can't we meet? Who has my heart? Where is the thief?

– Poor man!

– Unhappy soul!

– I hope for the poor fellow's sake that he never succeeds in meeting you!

– You know, my dear, only someone who has nothing to do can waste time listening to your fantasies.

– Pay no attention to her, Signor Perelà, her husband is one of the finest men in the Kingdom, a handsome man, healthy and strong, able to give her every legitimate satisfaction.

– Oh, the impossibility of understanding! From the soundness of my husband I have had nothing but brutality to which I have submitted out of duty.

– That's an exaggeration if there ever was one.

– If your husband had been sickly or feeble, my pretty one, or like Lady Gioconda's husband who isn't of any use, we would have heard you whining just as much for a vigorous one.

– Silly fools! Who among you has ever known love?

– Enough, for goodness' sake.

– We know only too well what Oliva is getting at.

– She's asphyxiatingly romantic.

– Always with that dangling heart of hers.

– Don't you see that Signor Perelà is getting bored?

– Let someone else speak.

– Yes someone else.

– Lady Giacomina!

– Yes, yes!

– Lady Giacomina!

Lady Giacomina Bàrbero di Ca' Mucchio

– And now the parable of the doughnuts!

– And the apotheosis of King Charles-Mini!

– Listen to this, Signor Perelà, it's enough to make you die with laughter.

– Be quiet, this Charles-Mini makes my flesh creep! I can't think about him without becoming nauseated.

– Lady Giacomina is the voice of experience.

– What will be new to you, Signor Perelà, is just a big bore to us.

– Certainly better than Oliva with her whining story. At least Lady Giacomina and Charles-Mini make us laugh.

– Will you ladies keep silent for a change?

– Be quiet, I said!

– Let her speak.

– There is an old proverb that says "not all doughnuts turn out with a hole." That, Signor Perelà, is gospel truth. Bakers who make doughnuts knead the dough very quickly and energetically and then put the doughnuts on a board side by side, ready for the oven. Although they are all perfectly equal in appearance, you can't tell how they will turn out. The baking, the greater or lesser consistency of the dough, the combined action of the yeast and the fire will cause the doughnuts to come out of the oven with significant differences. There will be some with a large round hole, in others it will be oblong, or oval or shaped like an 8. Others will turn out without any hole whatsoever – clogged. And finally, there will be one in which the hole is imperceptible, barely able to be seen and only if the doughnut is held up against the light. Only a single ray of light could penetrate it. My dear friend, nature, which everyone praises as a teacher of perfection, is not less liable to err than is the baker who makes doughnuts; and human beings, though they seem to be made all alike, hide unsuspected anomalies. Well then, that doughnut

through which only a ray of light could penetrate...
is me, Signor Perelà; I am that doughnut.

– Isn't that a good one?

– This little story makes me laugh so much.

– I can't stand this business about Charles-Mini!

– For goodness' sake, will you keep quiet, yes
or no? What a bunch of chatterboxes. Lady
Giacomina, how did you come to meet Charles-
Mini?

– It is with the voice of experience that I speak
to you, Signor Perelà. One month after my wedding, my marriage was annulled in the most
decisive manner by all the authorities. I was the
talk of the town, and I had to leave my beloved
country for a while. My good mother took me on a
voyage in order to distract me from my bewilderment. Occasionally I met someone who, because of
mutual attraction and youthful transport, seemed to
me suitable for making another try. Full of hope and
trust, yet trembling with doubt, I approached him.
Alas! You know full well, Signor Perelà, that it is
just when we are looking for something in
particular that we meet exactly with its opposite.
With my mother I visited France and Spain,
England, Germany, a part of Africa, India and
China, Russia; and I was preparing to cross the
ocean, dragging my misfortune throughout the
world, and at the same time ready to use the wealth
it was denied me to enjoy in a happier way. We
were in a picturesque mountain village where we
had gone to escape the summer heat when my
mother heard a washerwoman speaking of a certain
Charles-Mini. Without suspecting anything unusual
in this name, but aroused purely by curiosity, my
mother asked the woman who the man was and why

he was so called. The woman appeared so reticent
to answer that my mother, more and more curious,
pressed her with questions. "He has...my dear lady,
a thing...a thing, my dear lady..." said the woman
laughingly, but red in the face and full of embarrassment, while my mother urged her to explain, "a
thing that can't be mentioned...and that looks like
the little finger of a new-born babe." My mother,
who though dimly divining the truth did not expect
so surprising a revelation, gave such a loud cry that
she almost fainted. And the woman, having now
become bold, tried to soothe her: "He's a poor
wretch, an out-and-out wretch my dear lady; all the
women of the town keep making fun of him, and the
men even more so. At first he didn't realize his
misfortune, but now that everybody else knows it,
he knows it too, and he'll end by shutting himself
up in the Franciscan monastery." "No! No! No! He
must not cloister himself!" shouted my mother, running back and forth like a caged animal. "For
Heaven's sake, he must not enter the cloister," she
continued to shout in a frenzy. "Have Charles-Mini
brought to me at once, without a minute's delay, I
must see him at any cost..."

Without my knowing anything at all about it,
and without Charles-Mini knowing anything about
it, my mother arranged everything, and one morning
she led me to a lovely and solitary grove where she
left me alone, asking me to wait for her. In her
voice and in her behavior there was something odd
and mysterious that puzzled me, and she was
unable to conceal the nervous anxiety that troubled
her. In the sweet cool of the place, I stretched out
on a soft bed of leaves and waited. And soon, down
there at the forest entrance, two great branches

parted, like the curtains of a theater stage, and a very tall and fat young man, blond, with a rosy babylike face without a hair on it, appeared between them, as if by enchantment. From his looks he could not have been much more than twenty years old, perhaps the son of a small landowner of the village. He came toward me, and though he was ill at ease and trembling, exceedingly bashful, the imposing size of his body gave him a majestic air. When he was close to me, he asked in a thin, faint voice, such as I had never heard in anyone of either sex: "Is your good mother coming here?" "She will be here soon," I replied naïvely: "If you need anything you may wait for her." And still more embarrassed and trembling he lay down beside me. There he was, stretched out on the green, with an appearance that was masculine because of his awesome size, gigantic and yet extremely babyish at the same time. I can't explain it, but I too began to feel embarrassed, already invaded by that inexplicable and natural reserve that precedes the close contact between a man and a woman. His light blue eyes became dim; two heavy clouds descended upon his timid gaze. I was all flustered, and he even more so. My voice began to quaver, and his became increasingly thin – a silken thread. How often I had trembled when near a man, hoping with all the strength of my being...only to have it all end in a burst of laughter, bitter and obscene, in a cruel disappointment, in the most absurd of adventures. Charles was near me, all trembling, and I trembled with him. We would have thrown ourselves into each other's arms, but something held us back: what was it? Neither of us knew then what held the other back; we both were trembling with the same

61

anguish. How did we overcome it? I wouldn't be
able to say. After a few moments and a strange
languor, I awoke happy. I could hardly believe in
the miracle: I had known a man, and Charles had
found his woman. Through my mother, Providence
had intervened. And when it was accomplished, my
mother, who had remained hidden behind some
foliage so as to observe the scene, leaped out and
fell upon us, kissing and embracing the two of us.
"My children! Blessed children of mine!" she
repeated amidst her tears: "The Lord will bless
you, too! Angels of the Lord! Mother's angels!
Angels of Paradise! Angels of Earth!"

My first thought was to return to my native land,
but because of my consort's inferior social standing
and his highly unusual physique, I could not present
him to the Court or to society: Charles is the son of
a small hotel-keeper of that village. At first I
managed to keep the secret and could stroll undis-
turbed with my legitimate spouse; but since
everyone imagined all sorts of things about our
doings after the scandal of my first marriage, the
truth came to light, and the inevitable pranksters
wanted to carry him in triumph. He lives with me in
my palace or in one or another of my villas, far
from indiscreet eyes, and we sometimes take a
little trip together.

    – Ha! Ha! Ha!

    – To look at him he's a gorgeous man, big and
tall.

    – A colossus!

    – Yes, but a colossus of butter; he's all fat, he
doesn't have any muscle.

    – And he eats like a horse!

    – Such a stallion, what do you expect?

– Lady Giacomina takes good care of him...

– I'll bet she does. Where would she find another?

– Look here, Signor Perelà, if I didn't have such a good appetite, this matter of Charles-Mini would be enough to turn my stomach.

– Oh, you've got the stomach of an ostrich!

– It's a pity they don't have children.

– It really is.

– The race of the Charles-Mini!

– And of doughnuts without holes!

– No, my dear, the hole is there, but it's too small.

– Ha! Ha! Ha!

The Baroness Rosalinda Panciera, Widow Bon-Semblant

– In my status as a widow, Signor Perelà, I will say to you only that for a woman, widowhood is certainly the best condition. Three years after my marriage, Baron Bon-Semblant was killed in a hunting accident. As soon as I recovered from the fright and the grief that such an awful misfortune caused in me, and calm was restored to my soul, I discovered with perhaps even more astonishment an inexpressible relief from a condition of satiety and monotony of which I became aware only then.

– That's not hard to believe.

– Mine never goes hunting.

– Tell him to go fishing.

– It's not the same thing.

– One never knows, a dizzy spell...

– He swims like a fish.

– As long as a woman is a maiden, all eyes are on her: "What does she do and what doesn't she do. Where does she go and where doesn't she go! With whom does she go: she has a dozen at bay, but won't settle for any of them; she's a teaser, she's a flirt, she's not a serious girl." And as soon as she settles on one: "What a disgrace! She pounced on him. It's disgusting how she throws herself at him. She doesn't have any restraint. She doesn't know what modesty is. They go too far. At this rate if he hasn't yet had her, he soon will. She's already lost it. Who'll want her now? A girl who's lost her honor is finished. She'll come to a bad end. She's a lost woman." And when she finally marries, every association with a man who isn't her husband arouses suspicion and sets off gossip. "They're carrying on, and how. They're having fun. It's an affair. They have a trysting place; people have seen her going in; they've seen her coming out...." They know at what time she goes there and at what time she leaves. Or else: "he goes right to her house whenever he wants to and with absolute freedom. What brazenness! Shameless hussy! Her husband is a willing cuckold..." and there are howls of laughter at the poor fellow's expense. "The maid acts as go-between." If the husband is jealous or violent: "sooner or later we'll hear the pistol shot; you'll see what happens when he finds out about it...." And they do their best to make him find out. Until finally there comes the scandal that forms the joy of every evening party. And you know, my noble friend, that adultery is a crime for which the penal code prescribes a harsh punishment; even the Gospel brands it as infamous.

– Yes, but Jesus saved the adulteress when they wanted to stone her.

– You don't expect Jesus to go out of his way every single time a husband feels horns growing on his head.

– But in doing it for one, He did it for all. Jesus' intervention serves as an example; in fact, today we no longer stone anyone.

– If we were to stone every woman who strays, my dear, we would all have to busy ourselves with gathering rocks.

– Most people aren't very interested in a widow's behavior. When the door isn't barred one doesn't bother to count how many go in. All the specimens that a widow goes through in order to arrive at a second marriage are considered dull and boring stuff, colorless. "Will she have him or won't she? It seems so, it doesn't seem so. It's this time, for sure. It's about time! No way! It looked as though she'd marry him, but she's called it off. No matter; perhaps next time. Did she accept him? Not at all; she turned him down in the most polite manner." The second marriage takes place quietly, without any celebration. Nobody cares. And that's why, after twenty years as a widow, I still haven't made up my mind.

The Countess Rosa Ramino Liccio

– I was born clothed, Signor Perelà. Do you know all the mysterious meaning of this bewitching word: chastity? Doesn't it make you think of something that is ever so hidden and yet must forever stand before you in its absolute nakedness? When, as a girl, I was being educated in the convent, I used to be seized by a violent shuddering – a real fever – and by fits of the most vehement crying at the mere thought that a man might see the tip of my nose or the tip of my finger, the tiniest part of my wrist or neck, not to mention the rest. It was something I couldn't even think about, just the thought of it would have been enough to make me die. In the convent I did not wear the uniform – chaste though it was – worn by all the other girls, but rather a nun's habit which covered me more completely; and I would wrap bands around my head right down to my eyebrows and up to my lower lip, leaving uncovered only what was indispensable in order to live. I always wore gloves, too, and if anyone had to talk to me I would lower a very thick veil over my face. I'll not describe to you the enthusiasm of the virginal nuns in charge of my education and my care; they saw in me an example of that celestial purity which no one had ever succeeded in attaining and which it would be futile to claim or aspire to on earth. Indeed, Signor Perelà, I was born clothed!

When they removed me from the convent, they delivered me – I was but eighteen – into the arms of my fiancé Count Ramino, a lieutenant in the Cavalry. There is no way that I can tell you what I experienced during our amatory relations. Having understood my nature, my dear fiancé had me climb the ladder one step at a time, and yet I remained prey to the dizzy spells and terror caused by my extravagant chastity. He was obliged to violate it day by day, discreetly, with a patience and skill that only instinct can teach; and when I had become accustomed to one step, he would attempt the next one. What he had to endure in order to extort an

affectionate word or look from me, not to mention
a caress and the first kiss! And when we were
husband and wife he had to strive months and
months to obtain what all husbands obtain from
their wives on their wedding night. Only habit
could mitigate and allay my anguish. I was born
clothed in at least a thousand mantles, all of them
very light, impalpable, and with the sole purpose of
freeing myself from them.

In the first years, marriage removed so many of
those mantles from me that the hours passed always
new, whirling, exciting. But the day came when,
having become used to the last step taken, I did not
feel as in the past the proximity of a new one. My
husband did not succeed in removing another
mantle from me as he had always done. The poor
man made the greatest effort but was unable to
advance any further. He didn't know what to do, or
he couldn't do anything more. His mantles came to
an end there; he had arrived – naked. But as for me,
of the thousand I mentioned to you, I felt so many
still on me, perhaps six-or-seven hundred! Those
that in the beginning I wore so imperceptibly
because of their extreme lightness and impalpability, and which I had suffered to be torn from me
with such sweet violence, with anguish, now
weighed heavily upon me; they suffocated me, and I
felt myself oppressed and crushed by them as by
hundreds of leaden capes.

We were having coffee one day, and my husband
was lavishing upon me those habitual and ineffec-
tual caresses that I no longer felt. How tiresome,
how irksome upon one's skin a hand that has
nothing to say. He caressed my neck and my
forehead, and it was as though he had stroked the

surface of the table or the wood frame of a sofa. My husband's orderly knocked to carry out some duty or other. He entered. A thought flashed across my mind. I rushed to lock the door and, keeping the key, I went back to the sofa and embraced my husband. My eyes were again as they once were; he understood and resumed his caresses. Never had I suffered so much; I suffered as I did on the first day, and even more. What cruel anguish, what deathly shivers, what horror! Not until that day did I understand what a caress from my husband could do to me. The orderly ran to the door but couldn't open it. Bewildered and almost in tears, he took shelter in a corner of the room and watched in a daze to the very end. Meanwhile I was suffering all my shame; but those shivers that shook my slender body freed it of one mantle after another, just as a snake casts off its skin in the spring.

Thereafter my husband always invited the orderly. The good and simple rustic complied, embarrassed at first, then unembarrassed, then artful, malicious. He began to smile, contributing to the scene with little motions, with pointed gestures, salacious and obscene, with abusive words, insults, vicious shouts directed at me, and vulgar mimicry. I would stare at him, riveted, startled, horrified, entirely absorbed by his look and by his voice from which I drew the shame I desperately needed. I had picked up where I had left off, and the mantles continued to fall and fall from my body.

But the good and simple young man also reached his limit, and once again I began to feel upon me the weight of my unbearable clothing. Alas! His looks, his gestures and his insults could now produce in me only that boredom which for a woman is of the greatest annoyance.

Then it was a friend of my husband, a young captain, whom my husband asked for the secret favor. He would stay by the window smoking a cigarette or reading the paper, then turn around once in a while, unexpectedly, smiling with satisfaction. The way he looked at me! His eyes, warm and calm, in which I clearly read his judgment.... The mantles fell from me, scarlet with horror, one after another. But the obliging captain, too, soon exhausted his possibilities...and one day there were two of them. Signor Perelà, I feel that I still have many of these horrible garments on me, and I think with dread how I might rid myself of them; their weight increases every day, and I shall die suffocated beneath my implacable mantling.

– My dear, with your warped theory of mantles, I wouldn't be at all surprised to see you, one of these days, in the middle of the street not wearing any mantle at all.

– Who invented the sense of shame? The Lord in His infinite purity, or men in their boundless impurity?

– You, and you alone, have invented this fantasy for the sake of your nutty whim.

– Only animals let themselves be seen doing certain things!

– But animals don't have a sense of shame, and that's why they do it.

– And you are like them!

– Her husband was the finest young man ever known; what a handsome lad; you should see him, the most handsome of our officers, simple and wholesome.

– She debauched him!

– One can understand why he ended by enjoying it; he too became depraved.

– Why don't you invite Signor Perelà to watch?

– He looks shy enough to make a dozen of them fall from you all at once.

The Duchess Gelasia Del Prado Solìes

– To give you an idea of the different effects the same cause can produce, I shall speak to you, Signor Perelà, of the eyes of Bobì.

My illustrious family, as a consequence of foolish speculations and an unwarranted craze for grandeur on the part of my father and paternal grandfather, fell into a state of near-indigence and complete disarray; and it was to the great relief of all when, to improve our condition a little, I was given in marriage to the Duke Del Prado Solìes, an enormously wealthy man, sixty years old, a most notorious libertine full of ailments and fixations. I was then eighteen, and my consort, who at the beginning was tolerable enough, led me to a secluded life on his great estate of Albé where he hoped to restore his health, which by then was seriously impaired.

I was so utterly bored and resigned that I did not even think that when my venerable consort would die and leave me half of his fortune, I would still be in the full bloom of life to enjoy it.

He took a turn for the worse and could no longer leave the house. He continued to worsen and was confined to a very soft armchair, progressively disabled by the notorious paralysis that had seized him some years earlier, the direct result of the excesses and sins of his youth. Because he was jealous and suspicious, distrustful, he did not permit me to leave his side except for the very briefest moments. To soothe and distract him, I would read to him and read...and read...while at my feet lay Bobì, my lap-dog, dear and inseparable companion of my adolescence and now of my imprisonment.

The old man deteriorated and sent for his nephew, a lieutenant in the cavalry, who along with me was heir to the entire fortune. He arrived and graciously remained there in order to lend some cheer to that languishing life. We got to know one another. He would come and go; he would stay a few days, go away again and after a short while come back. His name was Silvio. He was twenty-six, a very handsome young man, tall and blond, with a lively disposition.

I would read and read and read...in his soft armchair the old paralytic would doze and doze and doze...his nephew would look at me and look at me and look at me...at my skirt hem Bobì would cuddle closer and closer and closer....And there happened what was bound to happen despite the fact that I was in a daze and in an absolute state of numbness: a current of sympathy, a current of love, a current of passion. But how to get away from the suspicious old man? Whenever one of us left, he would find an excuse to keep the other by his side; and when Silvio wasn't there, I couldn't leave him for a minute. Not even when he would depart was I allowed to accompany him to the gate of the villa; and I was obliged to eat and sleep next to my insufferable master. He was always dozing, but he never slept.

I had to resort to one of those stratagems that every woman guards jealously in the strong-box of her mind. I seized upon his pernicious insomnia to speak about it to the doctor in his presence, and the doctor prescribed a certain powder to be taken in warm liquid every evening before retiring. And in so saying, he wrote out the prescription.

I administered great quantities of that beneficent powder to my sleepless husband who, even in the middle of day, began to take the most beatific naps that anyone has ever enjoyed.

I would walk with Silvio in the garden, in the park, and in the woods of the villa, and precisely there in the deep green, where nobody might surprise us, we entertained ourselves.

On that natural carpet, so fresh, so soft and beautiful, among all those intertwining branches, I saw only the vast depth of two eyes that drew mine down the giddy cliffs of oblivion, down to the bottom, an unsoundable and limitless bottom, while my mouth was lost in a sweet cloud of silk and gold – for Silvio had a magnificent blond moustache.

Oh! this love, so new to me, vibrant, joyful, after so many hours given over to the old paralytic.

It's strange, but one day, in one of those moments when all of our faculties seem absorbed, the corner of my eye still managed to perceive Bobì: little Bobì, who never for an instant abandoned his adored mistress, lay stretched out a few inches from me, from my cheek, staring into my face with his large black eyes, fixed, round, entreating....It was a cold shower on the most passionate moment of my life. Silvio noticed, asked, inquired...but I would not explain my uneasiness to him. I did not wish to or I did not know how to. I was unable to. I couldn't explain it even to myself.

My husband endured for two more years on the edge of the abyss, but from that day on I didn't succeed in betraying him either with Silvio or with any other man. And after he died, for a long time it was impossible for me to approach any man. I was absolutely convinced that Bobì would have followed me and that I could not have rid myself of him without ruining everything.

Three years after my husband's death, my dear Bobì also died; he was nineteen years old, the unforgettable companion of my youth. Afterwards...I came to know other men, but at that particular moment...when all our faculties seem to succumb, memory remains alert and vigilant: there he is – Bobì, my dear Bobì, there he is, stretched out a few inches from me, from my cheek, with his large eyes wide open, fixed, entreating.

– Be honest, my dear Gelasia, you'd give all the lovers in the universe to be able to bring back your Bobì.

– Ah...perhaps.

The Princess Bianca Delfino Bicco Delle Catene

– If you have listened carefully to my good friends, Signor Perelà, you must have gathered that they consider love more or less an essential question of life. I was never able to think of it in that way, nor by myself could I recall a single detail. For me it was always a question of death: the point where life and death meet. Upon reaching it I lived in death and could remember nothing:

death in its luxurious blossoming of cold petals, in its astral void.

When, lying beside a man, I was being reborn to the light of day and my senses were gradually regaining their functions, my companion had already smoked one cigarette and would be lighting a second, he would be nonchalantly curling his moustache or calmly reading the newspaper. From the brink of the grave, still completely submerged, immobile and white, still a good three-quarters dead, I could dimly see his face, serene, content, satisfied, ruddy with health.

What had happened? How long had I been buried? Little by little I would disinter myself and come forth from the tomb, because, you see, I had truly died. I had felt my body's temperature fall to the zero point and a shudder slowly invade my every fibre and bone. I had felt my whole body stiffen and my skin contract in a final convulsion. I had entered into nothingness.

The offensive indifference, the cynical irreverence with which men treated my exceptional, no, my near-sacred sensitivity embittered me so greatly that I decided to withdraw into a contemplative solitude in my villa outside the city, where I still live. How could I have suffered next to me the pink animal, the coarse creature?

I lived solitarily. I complied with my obligations at Court and paid a rare visit to one friend or another. But I made frequent visits to the cemetery, my sole comfort and joy where my revered mother is buried in the family chapel and which, most fortunately, is but a very few steps from the villa.

Tirelessly wandering among the dead, I would think of their supreme moment.

I too...how many times I had died!

Wherein lay the difference?

That they had not yet been resuscitated.

In the evening I would walk along the path that skirted the walls of the villa and those of the cemetery. One evening I saw a young man of twenty go by, a delicate figure with an aristocratic and weary bearing, weary beyond description, with a spectral gauntness, his cheeks sunken and white, his eyes enormous within two black depths, his hair dark and curly, attractively disheveled, very luxuriant. A lad whose sensuous mouth seemed prematurely faded and who conveyed an air of dissipation and profound sadness. Not a ray of a smile on his lips or in the hauntingly beautiful eyes that lay within those dark caverns.

Fascinated, I gazed at him; and he gazed at me. Like him, I too was walking sorrowfully, with my air of a beautiful woman just disinterred.

The following evening the youth passed by again; he passed by evening after evening, always at the same hour, his gait more and more weary, his face whiter and whiter, his gaze staring out from an ever greater depth, while his mouth, so sensuous, seemed to me more and more faded. We looked at each other the way one looks at oneself in the mirror.

Once I went out in the dark of night, I don't know why; perhaps because of some strange premonition. There was a moon, and for the first time I was tempted to go out alone at that hour. I was invaded by anxiety...seized by an unknown disquietude....I was in need of a breath of air.

When I came to the gate, I noticed a shadow, a flat shadow silhouetted against the wall in front, and a blue face on which the moon had liquefied.

I stood motionless, and so did the shadow – the mirror!

The image in it approached imperceptibly, with the impalpability of motionless air, until it immersed itself in its stagnant pool of mercury. The cold liquid filtered through my mouth and made its way through all my veins, through all my fibres, through all my bones.

When I detached my lips from the mirror and opened my eyes, his were still half-closed; then he opened them quickly, fluttering them with the movement of a black and white butterfly, startled that he had remained so long in his reflection.

The young man had come to live, with his mother, in a villa not too far from mine, and from then on we met every night. Signor Perelà, I had found my love – after so much loneliness, after so much sacrifice, after so much sorrow...

But alas, the youth, who was dying, who knew how to die with his companion, seemed to me whiter each time, and his eyes blacker and blacker, larger and more beautiful in the deep of those dark cavities.

Suddenly he said to me: "Let us go down there... there's moonlight."

"Where, love? Yes, love." What wouldn't I have done to satisfy my youth's every wish? Through the fields we came to the low part of the cemetery wall. He helped me to climb over it, and we went down among the dead. He urged me forward with eagerness, he urged me on among the graves, side-stepping the crosses, passing among the little gates, the broken columns, the statues, the little flower beds, the shrubs, the pillars, looking at the lanterns that here and there threw a faint light on a black cross or on an old photograph. At a certain spot he halted; calmly he turned around smiling as in a moment of supreme joy, and then stretched out on the bare ground. I did likewise, and that night we were two corpses that the gravedigger had neglected to bury.

We returned night after night, lingering until very late.

Signor Perelà, I felt that a life had poured itself wholly into mine; I counted every single sip, terrified by the thought that each one might be the last.

One night my youth was whiter, whiter and colder. I died all the more; and as I began to revive and as the warmth returned to my body, I realized that he was still cold and motionless. His mouth had become like rubber against mine, which was reacquiring vigor and its normal temperature. I kept still. This had always happened to him. Now death was keeping him a little longer, a most natural thing. I waited yet a while. Poor little dear, my own little dear one; his joy was so great that each time he took longer and longer to revive. It seemed that he did not want to revive, so much did he love death. I waited. My angel, how great your happiness and your beauty. I waited...nothing. My body was once again animated and warm, while his became colder and colder. I gave a start. Was it a seizure? I caressed him, felt him, hugged him... nothing. I waited with an anxiety that became desperate. I waited, feeling myself invaded by an anguish that made me tremble all over; I waited...

nothing! But then...it was true...he had truly died...
this time.

I got up, turning around forsaken...the place...
the hour, my reason, which had returned to me completely, and the reacquired sense of reality – the
wretched, base, deceptive reality that does not
exist and yet crushes us – I was overcome by fear
and became terrified. I would have to explain his
death! Everybody saw me with him at night. They
would suspect me. And then...how could I flee,
leaving him there alone, my boy, my love? No...no,
I had to find a way! And frenzy drove me to take
him up in my arms. I lifted him up gently and I
hugged him again. I felt an unknown, superhuman
strength in me, and up...up...up....I scaled the wall,
placing him on top of it, and on...on...through the
fields...along the road...stopping only to summon
from my sinews new energy, every strength known
and unknown, on...on...driven by my exalted spirit,
on...on....I succeeded in dragging him home
without being seen, on...on...up the stairs,
embracing him, falling exhausted on the steps,
on...on...into my bed chamber...where I rested him
on my bed...and fell beside him, spent.

My strength came back a little, and my mind
allayed its fear, its foolish fear. Once safely inside
I looked at my white youth...his eyes half-closed in
the depth of the black wreaths on his beautiful face
that had become waxen. He reposed calmly, fixed
in the last moment of intoxication that I had given
him. An angelic air descended on that face which
was now composed in a celestial peace.

My boy had died, had died with me...for me...he
had truly died...down there....And I had taken him
away from his true place....Why had I brought him

away? Out of fear, for letting myself be led by a
phantasm: fear! But fear of what? Fear for myself? If
they had hanged me by the neck in the middle of the
square, I would not have died. Who could make me
die, now that my love was no more? He alone had
this power. I had wrenched him from his nest, where
he had wished to go that night, and where he had
always wished to return, to remain there every
night. I...who alone in the world had understood
him, had taken him from his realm; I had failed to
crown our love worthily, I had ruined all, profaned
all in a moment of bewilderment and madness.
Foolish woman! Mad woman!

I picked him up again, his arms dangling limply
over my shoulders, like a mother who picks up her
already-sleeping child to put him to bed, and away
again, down the stairs, through the garden, along
the road. I crossed the fields unseen, unheard. I
dragged him over the cemetery wall, and without
discomposing him, side-stepping the crosses, the
broken columns, the little gates, the shrubs, the
little flower-beds, I again reached his nest, ours,
and there where the grass was flat from his body, I
laid him out with devotion, safe, without feeling
broken – untired, unafraid. What or whom had I to
fear now that I had found my soul again? I stood
there erect before my destiny, erect over my boy.
Dawn was breaking.

– Bianca's story is both beautiful and terrifying,
is it not, Signor Perelà? One is left speechless by
it.

– One just doesn't know what to say.

– She always stops at this point, poor thing; just
as she did that morning.

– If you only knew, they came running to see her from the neighboring villages and from the city. She remained standing over her dead boy, like a statue, until the following night when the cemetery custodians made her leave by force.

– They had to pick her up and carry her away!

– And to those who had gathered there, she shouted: "I killed him! I've killed him! With my love!"

– At the top of her lungs.

– And she told all, from a to z.

– "Old bag! Shameless bitch!" they shouted all around her.

– The women couldn't get over it. They wanted to lynch her.

– "Slut!"

– "Cunt!"

– And even worse, Signor Perelà.

– *Tu te rappelles, mon ange?*

– For a long time she was on everybody's tongue.

– She went unpunished because she's related to important members of the Court and because the Royal Family's physician, in his official report, declared that Bianca Delle Catene is a splendid lady, but in that particular matter definitely cracked.

– There were those who wanted to punish her, all the same.

– That young man's mother.

– But he was already diseased!

– Galloping consumption!

– A rotting mass!

– He was already a corpse when Bianca first met him on that moonlit night.

– Otherwise she wouldn't have taken to him, that's certain...anyone even a little bit healthy, how revolting!

– Every night, Signor Perelà, I go out, I stop at the gate, I cross the road, the fields, I scale the wall, and there where my boy lies I stretch out to restore to him his last moment of life. We are as we were then. I die at that moment while he relives the supreme moment of our love. I am but the vessel of this relic.

– Who is it that hasn't yet spoken?

– That spiteful Nadina.

– Enos, Enos hasn't said a word!

Mlle. Enos Copertino

– Enos Copertino, the greatest pianist in the Realm, decorated by the King and Queen!

– Signor Perelà, it's useless to question her; the great artist has never opened her heart to anyone. She wouldn't answer you.

– She lives with Catulva, the famous tragedienne.

– Enos likes to keep her mouth shut, but people open theirs for her too.

– She lives in a mysterious villa where no man has ever entered, where no man can enter, and among women only Catulva. She appears exclusively by order of the King, and only to play the piano.

– They say that at night two phantoms wearing endlessly long gowns can be seen wandering in her garden. They are glimpsed clasped together, now here now there, while on the veranda two nimble white hands play a Chopin nocturne. But nobody can say anything about her; nobody knows a thing.

God

– Like you, Perelà, I think of those three women. I am at the top of a chimney and I hear them talking. Their loving whispers absorb all my senses, and I can neither see anything nor move my limbs even a little. They talk of human suffering. Of the three who is speaking? Is it *Pena*? Is it *Rete*? Is it *Lama*? One tells of a heart's pain. One spreads the net that ensnared it. One carries in her hand the blade that will pierce it.

– *God.*

– I hear them, I hear them, I hear them! And I do not know what drives me to single out something specific about each of them. Tell me, tell me, Perelà, what did you long to see, what did you long to know of your three mothers? What was it that most struck your imagination, your fantasy, or what was it that you felt you had best surmised about them?

– The eyes of *Pena,* the hands of *Rete,* the smile of *Lama.*

– Look into my eyes, observe my hands and my smile. At this moment I feel that I am the sum of all those things!

– *God.*

– Tell me, then, did you think that the Queen had different eyes, different hands, and a different smile? To be sure, the ladies of society must have agreeably entertained you yesterday, but I...what can I do? I can do nothing. I am the Queen, and the Queen is alone.

– *God.*

– The Queen cannot search her past or her heart, which does not belong to her. And when she probes the future, alas, you see her pick up a blood-stained sword...and disappear. But I can teach you a Queen's game, the one called Statecraft.

– *God.*

– Here now, this is the deck of cards. These are the *Dames;* you hold them. And these are the *Knights.* I hold the *Kings.* The *swords* here. You shuffle the *Dames,* I shuffle the *Knights.* You shuffle the *coins,* I the *swords.* The *Kings* on this side. I pick a *Knight,* you pick his *Dame.* And now one of the *coins.* The *Knight* that pairs with the highest *coin* becomes *King* in the world where money rules. The matching *Dame* is the *Queen.* Now then! This is the *King,* and this his *Queen;* the money goes to the State. Shuffle the *King* with the *swords;* when the *King* pairs with the highest *sword,* he dies.

– And if they don't pair?

– As long as they don't pair he reigns.

– And then?

– I've already told you, he dies.

– *God.*

– There's more, there's more. This *King* has a long reign. Torlindao has a good forecast. But now it has happened: the *King* is dead, his *Queen* picks up that *sword* and disappears. Put her at the end of the table.

– And the *coin?*

– *Coins* belong to to the State, that doesn't change. And now the new *King* with the *swords,* until he pairs with the highest *sword.* The *Queen* picks up that *sword* and disappears. Put her there, at the end of the table.

– How does this game end?

– This game never ends.

– *God.*

– New Kings are made, new hearts to be pierced, new swords, new coins, new Queens who are left with a blood-stained sword.

– *God.*

– Your Majesty, several times I have heard a word spoken. I turned around but couldn't see...

– A word?

– *God.*

– Oh! Pay no attention to it. I have become so used to it that I don't even notice it. Come, there, it's my parrot; he's on the window sill, look. How beautiful he is. I was unable to teach him a single thing. He refused to learn anything from me. He has retained this one word that he heard, who knows how...and he always repeats it. It's strange, isn't it? He says only one word, but it is the greatest of all, and he cannot understand its meaning. Poor creature, how can you expect him to know what God is!

– But instead you do know.

– Of course! Certainly. Who doesn't know? God! Why God is...God. We all know, but the parrot.... Now you will accompany me on my ride in the Royal Park. The sun is about to set. Come, the carriage is waiting for us.

– Your Majesty, all those *Queens* that you made me put at the end of the table with the *swords,* the *Queens* of the dead *Kings*...

– There they are. They are at the other end of the Royal Park. Look at them. How wearily they drag their mantles of sorrow that cover them entirely. Look at how they are veiled, only the whiteness of their hands and faces can be discerned. In their right hand they carry the bloodied sword.

– And do they always roam about in here?

– They live in this damp and shadowy park, cemetery of the living. They are always out, wandering night and day along the iron fence that encloses them.

– And don't they devour one another?

– Why should they? Aren't they all equal in there? Were they not Queens, all? And do they not all have the same mantle and the same veil? Me alone they devour with their looks, and as soon as they see me they point with a fierce mien at the entrance to the enclosure.

– Tomorrow, perhaps, that gate will open again....Every evening the Queen comes to visit them at sunset. There are young ones among them, and old ones. Queen Cleofe has been there for fifty years; she is the Doyenne.

– Do they hate or do they love?

– They hate the swordless Queen. They love the memory of their King. They drag the sword that pierced his heart.

– What did they look like to you, my dear Perelà?

– A cage of big black birds whose wings have been cut off.

The Ball

– How wonderful it was!

– What a spectacle!

– I had never seen one quite like it.

– What?

– The pageantry, for goodness sake.

– Good evening, my dear.

– Good evening.

– Good evening, Gelasia.

– I won't kiss you, because I'd leave a smudge on you.

– *Adieu, mon ange.*

– Good evening, Nadina.

– You're here already?

– Welcome, darling.

– Is Zoë here?

– We haven't seen her yet.

– She was in the second carriage.

– It was really wonderful!...Wonderful! Wonderful!

– Really and truly wonderful.

– Would you believe it? I couldn't find room in any of the carriages. I had to take a cab from the square and go to my cousin Papavero's house to see something from her window. They went by twice, and when he was just below me I was so moved that, not knowing what to do, I took three red carnations I was wearing on my bosom and threw them down to him. He looked up at me and made the most gracious smile. Just for me, can you imagine? I felt a lump in my throat; I cried, oh, how I cried!

– I felt like embracing him in the middle of the street!

– Have you caught Rosa's malady?

– What a celebration!

– And what magnificence!

– Like the coronation of a King.

– Indeed.

– And the curiosity of the people.

– Incredible!

– And he, what dignity!

– What aplomb!

– What self-possession. The self-possession of a King!

– Let's admit it, you don't see it very often... like a true King.

– And to think that until just a few days ago he was inside a chimney cowl.

– Who would think so?

– It's really a miracle!

– I was afraid someone might take a shot at him.

– Nonsense! He's so well-loved, so respected, so adored by everyone.

– Standing in his carriage, he waved so graciously, so graciously...

– What elegance!

– Fascinating!

– *Quel charme!*

– Did you notice when the young girls threw flowers at him?

– What beautiful smiles they gave him!

– Such innocent smiles.

– And he...with his gray smile...

– Isn't that so?

– I thought they had thrown something filthy at him.

– You always think the worst.

– It wouldn't have been the first time.

– Do you remember Iba?

– What's Iba got to do with it? Do you want to compare Signor Perelà and Iba?

– I respect Iba much more.

– Because you're a fool!

– And a wicked person!

– Arrogant!

– Spiteful!

– You've simply decided to be different, expecting that everyone would give you their attention. But you're mistaken, my dear girl, we've got better things to think about, much better.

– What a nuisance she is!

– Odious!

– If I were Perelà, I'd fill her mouth with smoke and choke her.

– Tell me something. What if someone had really taken a shot at him?

– That's just what I was thinking. Probably it wouldn't have done him any harm.

– Right. Because being of smoke…

– Since he's made of smoke, the bullet would have gone through him intact.

– And it probably would have hit someone else.

– For heaven's sake, my husband was in front of him.

– What a thought, darling, can't you see that they love him? I heard the comments of people in the street. They all love him! Between you and me, the King would like to be loved that way.

– The wonderful thing is that now everyone finally believes in him.

– Everyone, you know!

– That's right, because at first many people had doubts.

– On hearing that he's made of smoke...

– But now that they have seen him...nobody any longer has doubts about him.

– Naturally.

– Everyone, everyone loves him, there's only that stupid Nadina who's hostile toward him.

– Who knows why?

– She does it to attract attention, don't you understand? Don't you know what that woman is like?

– The silly goose!

– And we'll pay no attention to her, then you'll see how she feels.

– In a few moments they'll be here.

– They took him all the way out to the country-side, so that everyone could see him.

– Even the peasants have hung lights from their windows.

– I'll never forget the pediment of Calleio Gate with all those lavender-colored Chinese lanterns, and there in the middle, in gray lanterns, the name – *Perelà*.

– How elegant!

– How exquisite!

– A dream!

– A fantasy!

– A fairytale!

– Of course, because when he arrived he entered by that gate.

– Oh, really?

– What, didn't you know? He entered through Calleio Gate, that's why they wrote his name over it. As of today it's no longer Calleio Gate, but the Gate of Perelà.

– Do you know what they're saying in the antechamber?
– What?
– They say this will be the last time that we have him among us.
– Why?
– Why?
– Why?
– He must go into seclusion to concentrate on the Code.
– That's all we needed, the Code!
– Now that we've found such a darling man, right away they take him away from us.
– For another of their silly affairs!
– Those darn papers that never resolve anything.
– But this is important, you know, it's our country's new Code!
– Our laws are so outdated and decrepit that it's a real disgrace!
– Have they definitely entrusted it to him?
– Positively!
– Third member.
– The King and the Minister will add their signatures below Perelà's.
– Third member.
– They won't be able to object to a single one of the articles he dictates.
– Third member.
– But how will he manage to get the necessary information?

– What kind of information?

– What do you mean by that?

– In some things he strikes me as being so naïve...

– That's just what's needed, to do things right, you have to be pure, otherwise we're back where we started.

– Naïve...oh, sure! He's probably more cunning than a fox. Those old women must have taught him where the devil keeps his tail, it's just that he's extremely reserved, and he's right to be so.

– He's anything but naïve, he doesn't want to waste his breath on you, that's all.

– And now he's going into seclusion in order to concentrate.

– And that's the end of that!

– What a shame!

– Do you know what we need to do?

– What?

– Beginning this evening we mustn't lose sight of him.

– Why is that?

– What do you think? We can exercise a lot of influence on him, a way for us to have a say in the Council of State.

– But how?

– If he were to fall in love with one of us?

– But the fact is he can't fall in love.

– Who told you so? Smoke or no smoke he's still a man. We can work on him so that he'll write whatever we wish.

– That's true. I hadn't thought of it.

– Besides, isn't he to dictate the Code's articles?

– That's true, that's true...

– He can dictate whatever he likes, and you can write down whatever you like.

– Third member.

– Do you understand?

– What do you think about it?

– The trouble is he can't fall in love, you see, he doesn't eat, he doesn't drink, he doesn't sleep...he doesn't do anything, the blessed fellow, he doesn't even sit down.

– What an indifferent man!

– He's made of smoke.

– How can one be so utterly insensitive?

– He's extremely sensitive when he wants to be.

– I've heard that Catulva is going to perform in his honor.

– *La Dame aux Camelias.*

– And Enos Copertino is going to play during the intermissions.

– Chopin's *nocturnes.*

– Do you like my *toilette*?

– How darling! Those three roses are exquisite, so becoming on you. And what do you think of my outfit?

– *Un rêve.*

– It's so simple.

– But it makes you look so young...fifteen, I'd say!

– Which is just half my age.

– That's all?

– *Que tu es méchante!*

– Have you seen George?

– How punctual he is!

– I insisted that he arrive ten minutes before me.

– Why?

– Haven't you noticed that when he enters, I'm already in the hall?

– I hadn't noticed it.

– It's scandalous!

– I'll pay attention next time.

– Everyone notices it, he doesn't know how to pretend.

– And how are things now between you and Frederick?

– Don't talk to me about it! The two of them are driving me mad. They'll be the death of me.

– What are you saying?

– George wanted to challenge him to a duel.

– George?

– I wouldn't hear of it.

– I should think not.

– After all, what if they actually kill one another? I need them, mind you! both of them.

– You're quite right.

– But George is like a child, a child that deserves to be spanked!

– What a naughty mommy!

– *Pe...perepè...pepepè. Pe...perepè...perepè... pepè!*

– Ah!

– Ooh!

– Here they are!

– They're coming!

– They've arrived!

– The carriage has entered the courtyard!

– My God!

– Viva! Viva!

– Viva Perelà!

– Perelà! Perelà!
– Viva!
– Beautiful! Beautiful!
– Long live the great Perelà!
– The One and Only!
– The divine one!
– My God!
– Viva! Viva!
– How exciting!
– My legs are shaking!
– I'm ready to faint!
– Viva!

– Silence!
– Make them be quiet!
– How moved he is!
– How happy he is!
– To me he always looks the same.
– Silence!
– The Minister is about to speak!
– My God!
– Silence!
– Your Excellencies, noble ladies, and illustrious sirs here assembled, I have the very high honor of announcing to you that in accordance with the proposal of the Supreme Council, by virtue of a Royal Decree, and with the approval of our Most Eminent Cardinal-Archbishop, the task of devising the new Code for our beloved Realm is entrusted wholly...
– Ooh!
– Sole member.
– to this superior, chivalrous creature, to this exceptional superhuman being that is Perelà.
– Ah!

– Sole member.

– What man of frail flesh and feeble senses could venture upon such an undertaking without fear of falling into those inevitable injustices that are unconsciously dictated to us by our blood, by our ambitions, by our private interests and those of our faction? What man could venture upon this immense labor confident of having forgotten that he too is a man and that as a man he shares the same personal concerns, the same selfish aims as do all those for whom the Code is to be prescribed?

He is not a man, or rather, he is the man whom the purifying flame enveloped so as to annihilate the turbid travail of matter...

– Well said!

– Bravo!

– Sole member.

– One and only!

– Is he not the sublimation of the body and of the human spirit? Does he not come among us to bear palpable testimony of other lives, of other times, of other destinies, of a life and destinies in which human instincts have no more sway?

Shall we then not offer thanks to Divine Providence for having sent him to us in this critical moment, precisely when we have been called upon to weigh our conscience with enlightened impartiality in order to establish a just measure by which to weigh and judge the conscience of each of us? And has Divine Providence not sent him to us that we might acknowledge this new, immense favor? Were we to fail to do so, we would feel that we were the most ungrateful of her children.

We thank thee, beneficent Mother, who in the hour of our greatest charge hast willed to come to our aid. We thank thee and vow to make ourselves worthy of thy favors and of thy messenger.

– Bravo!

– Well said!

– Long live the Minister!

– He, vital being, who knows the most hidden secrets of life, knows not life's material needs, or is scarcely aware of them. He, a being of thought alone, of spirit alone, does not disdain but rather gladly deigns to use on our behalf this thought, the noble labor of so great a spirit.

– Bravo!

– Viva Perelà!

– Long live the Minister!

– Sole member.

– One and only!

– From him we can expect only a work of purity and fairness, a work of absolute social justice, both material and spiritual.

– Well said!

– Bravo!

– Viva!

– A special committee will be nominated to accompany Signor Perelà wherever he deems appropriate. At his approach every door will open. He will visit the most secluded corners of our land, explore, command, inquire, interrogate, examine; then he will withdraw from all company for a period of meditation and concentration in order to undertake the awesome task.

– Viva!

– Viva Perelà!

– Long live the Minister!

– Hurrah for the new Code!

– Hurrah for the Code of Perelà!

– Viva! Viva!

– What a dear man you are!
– I was in the second carriage, didn't you see me? Look, some young girls had a few roses left, and they threw them to me. Here they are. Didn't you see me?
– Did you see me at my cousin Papavero's window? You did, didn't you? How sweetly you smiled at me! Do you know that I cried? I couldn't help it, I was so moved. I was simply overcome.
– And so...starting tomorrow you too will have your concerns, your worries.
– Our men, always so busy, have found something for you to do, too.
– They did it just to take him away from us.
– He was the one man on whom we could count...
– And they...nothing doing!
– Pigs!

– What a crowd!
– My God!
– I'm beginning to perspire.
– It's so hot...
– *Quelle chaleur!*
– I've never seen the Royal Palace in such a bustle as it is this evening.
– Do you know what I think?
– What?
– A lot of uninvited people must have made their way in. You see such strange faces around...
– You'd think we were in the public square.
– Naturally, there are always people who take advantage of these hulabaloos.

– Look! Look!

– Oliva!

– The Marchesa di Bellonda!

– Ooh!

– Dressed in gray!

– Smoky gray!

– What a fabulous idea!

– And to think that she never stands out at any party.

– How pretty she looks this evening!

– I too have a gray gown.

– But hers is brand new...

– How the dickens did she do it?

– The dressmakers were at her house working on it all night and all day today. The drawing-room was turned into a workshop, and the gown was finished ten minutes ago; don't you see how late she arrived?

– It suits her so well!

– She can compete with Zoë.

– Zoë is making a poor showing this evening, with that red dress.

– You know how that woman is. Provided not one degree of her useless curves gets lost, she's ready to ruin all the gowns in the world.

– But Oliva! Oliva!

– I have a magnificent gray boa.

– Nobody wears them nowadays, they're all right for our grandmothers.

– That doesn't matter, it would have been a good idea to dig it out for this evening.

– I have a gray and silver gown, but it's so *fanée*. Last year I wore it all season long.

– Do you want to know something? I'll have a hat made in the shape of a smokestack, with some

gray feathers coming out of the top, like puffs of smoke.
– Brava.
– And I'll dig out my boa.
– I want my smokestack for the evening of Catulva's performance.
– Look, look, she's going up to Perelà.
– And he, how he greets her!
– With what grace!
– He's taking her by the arm.
– The smoky couple!
– How adorable!
– Truly!
– They make a good pair.
– She with her big rosy face...
– A rose lost in the clouds.
– But she's made-up, you know, she's all painted!
– I'll say she is, she's always as green as a cucumber.
– How cute they are side by side!
– Did you see who had a bright idea this evening?
– Who would have thought so?
– A spark of genius!

– How ravishing you are, dear Oliva.
– Really?
– Yes, really.
– Your eyes are different.
– It's true.
– And your smile...you look like a different woman.
– How did you do it?
– What an exquisite idea you had.
– Nobody else thought of it.

– Why, you're the only one dressed in gray.

– And he.

– But he...he had no choice.

– Just the color needed for the occasion.

– It will become the rage, without doubt.

– It already has.

– I didn't do it for myself, you know. Not at all! But rather to pay him this small homage; I think he deserves it. I didn't invent a thing, I merely copied him...his color, I couldn't do any better than that. And if anybody wants to follow me, she may be sure that she'll be imitating him alone...to do him the honor he deserves.

– You did well!

– Brava.

– Truly.

– Did you hear that?

– With what rapture she spoke!

– But has she gone mad?

– Mad? She's in love.

– That famous dangling heart that she was always looking for...

– Is Perelà's.

– A heart of smoke.

– No wonder she couldn't find it.

– She's always been a little bit loony.

– How are you?

– So, so.

– Your face is so drawn

– You look waxen.

– It's the morphine.

– You wretch!

– I know.

– Do without it!

– Three injections last night.
– That's madness!
– I know.
– Think of Perelà.
– Perelà...

– Hello, my friend.
– Greetings.
– What are you up to?
– Me? Nothing. And you?
– I'm counting the chairs. At parties I always have this job. There's supposed to be one chair less than there are guests. Look, nobody is sitting down. They all think that the missing chair is the one meant for them. And when they get home they say they're tired.
– Is there a chair missing at this ball?
– I believe so.
– It's mine, I never sit down.
– Oh, of course. You're right. I had forgotten. You've brought perfection even to social balls.

– A delicate expression...delicate figure...
– A melancholy smile of nature.
– *Mignonne créature.*

– Tell me honestly, Signor Perelà, are you really a man like all the others?
– Without doubt, most illustrious Lady, except that I'm infinitely lighter than the others.

– Certain things...made of smoke....Ah! How I despise you!

– He sleeps standing up and doesn't get tired.

– Did you notice how Perelà's mustache is curled?

– Like the whim of a burning cigarette.

– How ingenious!

– What, pray tell, is this putrid flesh of ours?

– I wanted to take a turn with him, but he doesn't dance.

– Why not?

– What do you expect, he's already thinking about the Code. These dolts have taken him from us.

– And it won't be long before he puts on airs.

– It's inevitable.

– Like all the others.

– You'll see how stuffy he becomes.

– Three mothers?

– And...fathers, how many?

– You silly thing!

– But of course: a sparrow's tiny ass.

– Do you know what Perelà told me?

– What?

– "You seem so very very light to me, almost as light as I am."

– What a darling he is!

– What a dear.

– I don't know what it is about that man's eyes, I can't look straight at him.

– He's disturbing.

– It's true, that's the word, that's the exact word
– disturbing, disturbing.

– He is disturbing.

– Believe me, when I'm in his presence and he says that he feels so very, very light, I myself feel as though I'm rising. And note that I weigh three hundred pounds, but it doesn't matter....I feel myself going up...up...up....Without doubt the universe is supported by a feather.

– But he really is a man, you know, absolutely normal.

– A man? He is *the* man, you mean, with a capital M.

– The one that Diogenes was in search of?

– In person.

– Tell me, now: when did anybody ever see, before this evening, someone show up at a Court party in a pair of hunting or riding boots?

– They're so beautiful!

– And they look marvelous on him.

– And so polished...

– Who could be polishing them so well for him?

– He himself must be the bootblack.

– Oh, sure, you must be joking!

– It would really be something if they weren't even polished.

– As for me, I'd take him even if his boots were splattered with mud.

– I detest dirt!

– You can be sure that he'll drag dirt along even with polished boots. Who is he? Where did he pop out from? What sort of name is that? Perelà. Isn't that great? Ha! Ha! Ha! Ha!

– Yes, yes, as you wish, whatever you wish, as long as you don't bother us.

– Right! You're free to think as you like, but let us be.

– How obnoxious she is!

– I feel like gouging her eyes out!

– Will he succeed?

– Certainly, he'll succeed.

– No doubt about it.

– First Christ, and now Perelà.

– *Olì olì olà.*

– Right, right.

– Do you see these delicately colored playthings? Don't they seem like so many little angels to you? All covered with flowers, with gems...with veils....Well, listen, each one of those gems that they wear on their soft rosy skin, each one is the eye of a crime. I always say to them: you traps of human eggs. They take it and swallow it, because they're afraid I might say something worse.

– Signor Perelà, you must not speak with that fellow, absolutely not. He's not the sort of friend you need. It's already the second time that I've seen you together. He's a bad character! Everyone complains about him, everyone knows he's useless and treacherous, but nobody dares to drive him away. He goes around claiming to be a philosopher, but it's not true, pay no heed to him, he's an awful character, a vicious tongue, that's what he is! He says the most scurrilous things, none of them true, about us women because he's as ugly as a baboon and not one of us has ever deigned to look at him. And we have to put up with it all for fear he might say even worse things.

– The laws are there, it's just that no one respects them.

– Right.

– Will he succeed?

– *Olì olì olà!*

– One can't do too many things.

– And yet they get done.

– Tell me something.

– What is it, nuisance?

– Hasn't anybody noticed that that filthy creature has been here an hour and still hasn't removed his hat?

– Nadina, what a profound observation you've just made!

– What did she say?

– She says that Perelà hasn't removed his hat.

– Ha! Ha! Ha!

– Stupid!

– Let her talk. It's good that she makes stupid remarks, that way everyone can see what kind of woman she is.

– The King!

– The King!

– His Majesty!

– Viva!

– Long live the King!

– Viva Torlindao!

– Long live our King!

– The Queen!

– The Queen!

– Her Majesty the Queen!
– Viva!
– Long live the Queen!
– Viva! Viva!
– The Queen smiled at Perelà.
– What a gentle smile she gave him!
– With such grace.
– She smiled sweetly at him.
– Yes, but with a veil of melancholy.

– Perelà did not see the King.

– But is it true, Signor Perelà, that you didn't see the King?
– No, most illustrious Lady.
– He was the one who all alone formed the second row. First came two gentlemen of the Court, then he and right behind him was my husband.
– The one who was wearing the yellow sash is your husband?
– No, that was the King, my husband had a green sash. Listen, listen, Perelà thought that the King was my husband!
– Ha! Ha! Ha!
– He didn't see the King!
– But you did see how the Queen smiled at you.
– And who doesn't smile at you?

– *Olì olì olà!*
– Right!

– My friend, is it true that you didn't see the King?
– No, my dear fellow.

– I didn't see him either. How can one see him? He's surrounded by so many people....He no sooner comes in through one door than he leaves by another. Which one? You never know through which door the King enters and through which one he will exit. Today it's this one, tomorrow that one. The next day you think he'll change again, but not in the least, he goes out by the same one.

– But can he be afraid here, in his own house?

– In his own house! Do you call this a house? My dear fellow, who assures you that one of these little angels won't get him to sniff a little angelic bouquet; they love flowers so much that they put them everywhere! He would only need to pause a few minutes at the *buffet*. At Court Dinners the King doesn't eat, he prefers to converse with the gentleman on his right or with the lady on his left, and so he sends them home on an empty stomach. Of course he has eaten earlier, whereas the others, poor devils, must wait to fill themselves up later. And there you have a Court Dinner.

– The *buffet* rooms are open.
– Perelà! Perelà!
– Where is Perelà?
– Come and have some refreshments.
– Oliva! Oliva!
– Offer your arm to Perelà.
– A smoky couple!
– What a nice pair they make.
– Long life for smoke!
– May there always be smoke!

– Let me have the first bottle!
– *Pop!*

– Over here! Over here!
– *Pop!*
– To the health of Perelà!
– *Pop! Pop!*
– Viva Perelà!
– *Pop!*
– *Pop!*
– Long live the Minister!
– *Pop!*
– Viva Torlindao!
– *Pop! Pop!*
– Long live the Queen!
– *Pop! Pop! Pop!*
– Hurrah for the new Code!
– Sole member!
– Hurrah for the Code of Perelà!
– *Pop!*

The Visit to Sister Mariannina Fonte
And Sister Colomba Mezzerino...

In the courtyard of the Royal Palace a carriage awaits. Perelà, followed by three gentlemen of the Court, embarks on the first tour of inspection.
– *Signor Perelà.*
Inspector General of the State, reformer of men, of things, of institutions, and of customs. With executive powers material, spiritual...et ultra –
So reads the pass that has been issued to Perelà, which bears the signature of King Torlindao, and a little piece of which can be seen protruding from the boot of his left leg, like the petal of a rose.

As Perelà is about to take his place in the carriage, Alloro approaches: he is the Royal Palace's oldest servant, put at Perelà's personal service. Without being observed, he hands him a letter.

The carriage moves off at a trot, and Alloro, with a smile of admiration and devotion that brightens his whole person, watches it disappear. He continues to repeat to himself these words: "How has he managed to do it? How did he do it? Of smoke. It's hard to believe one's own eyes."

"Signor Perelà, do you remember me? I am the Marchesa Oliva di Bellonda. You may recall that a few days ago, along with my dear friends, I spoke to you of my poor soul. They interrupted me and objected to my words of discouragement and to my just grievances. I reproach them, you understand, neither for malice nor for spitefulness, but for ignorance, because only out of ignorance did they

109

reject my complaints. The poor things live with the illusion of loving and of being loved, of having loved, and they feel sure, may God forgive them, that what they talked about so lightly and so foolishly is love. Alas! I am she...who never has loved. Do you remember?

"I sought to embellish my words for you, and like my dear friends perhaps I spoke to you with affectation. I said to you: each of us, when born, bears within his breast someone else's heart, a maiden the heart of a youth, and the youth that of a maiden...do you remember? And that may well be so. Just think, then, how terribly difficult it is to meet that other person during our fleeting lifetime. Alas, it's true, we all end up bearing within ourselves this organ which has become of no use to us, this piece of flabby matter which, little by little and without our noticing it, becomes in our breast a sponge soaked with pain. It is the tragedy we all bear without realizing it, this may also be so...but today I no longer speak to you in that fashion, today I speak to you in quite another way, and with the utmost candor and simplicity I say to you: I have never loved till now because I had not found the man that could be loved by me. Moreover, today I could not even use such imagery or that tone of voice, I do not need to color my words. Two days ago I was unhappy, and now I am not. I love you.

"I have been told that you neither eat nor drink nor sleep, that you do nothing of what all other men do, and that one should not expect anything of you. Well then...since Friday, when I saw you, I have been as you are: I too have stopped doing anything, I have done nothing but think of you.

"You are thirty-three years old, are you not? So am I. I too am thirty-three. Thirty-three years ago you were put up there in your chimney, just when I was born. Had you continued to live since then, today you would be sixty-six years old, would you not? Twice my age. You would be...an old man, a man nearing death. And perhaps you would already be dead. Instead no, you are still young, a handsome young man, as young as I am and, like me, restored to life and new to love.

"I ask but one thing of you in return for all my love, one word: tell me that mine is not madness, but that you went up there to wait for me. It was to wait for me that you stopped half-way, to give me the time needed to reach you. I was so far away, so far away...and tired. I was running breathless, panting, desperate, exhausted; I was dying without hope of being able to reach you and bring you what of yours I possessed. But...you were good to me, so good and generous, you waited for me...and now here I am. I was able to reach you, I have reached you.

"The sublimely pure expression of your face is before me and says to me: 'I am of smoke.' So be it. Do you perhaps believe that this is a barrier that will block the way of the Marchesa Oliva di Bellonda? Do you believe that I might repeat any of the remarks made against you by my friends concerning your exceptional nature? What does that matter to me? You are made of smoke? I also am of smoke. I love you, and one who loves must ask for nothing, but only and always give, give, give...give always. To ask is to love oneself and not to love. You are so very light? I am as light as you, for I have rid myself of all suffering.

"My love has blossomed. And if the shower of its warm petals be welcome upon your fair brow and over the rest of your spiritual person, if indeed the warm petals of my love be not displeasing to you...if you do not refuse them...then know that my heart is a world for you, a world made all of gardens.

"You need not answer me, you shall never tell me whether you have loved me. It is not this that I wish, for were you to hate me, I would love you, were you indifferent to me, I would love you, were you to love me, I would love you. I have written to you for one reason alone: that woman who made you listen to her grief, who showed you her face full of pain, who told you she was unhappy, today no longer speaks that way, she no longer complains. She has another face; her lips have learned to smile, and her heart overflows with joy. That woman is happy. And it is only right that you should know why."

    – Here is Sister Mariannina Fonte, a sinner.
    – How many times have you sinned, Sister Fonte?
    – Three times, Signor Perelà.
    – And now you ask forgiveness for your sin?
    – Three times a day.
    – And what is sin?
    – Sin is what we must not do.
    – Not even when it gives us pleasure?
    – That is just when sin is worse.
    – And is the pleasure of men always sinful?
    – When it is not the pleasure of virtue. And here is Sister Colomba Mezzerino.
    – A penitent?

– A sinner she is not, Signor Perelà. Sister Colomba has brought us the fragrance of her purity, and she preserves it, for it is the fairest flower of all. She prays for sinners.

– There are, then, two kinds of persons: those who ask forgiveness for their own sins, and those who implore forgiveness for the sins of others.

– And a third kind, Signor Perelà: those persons who only sin. For them Sister Colomba, the chosen, prays night and day. Go, Go, Sister Colomba and implore mercy for those persons. I shall guide you through the convent, Signor Perelà. Only you may enter.

Ala

– Do men die at the worst moment of their lives, or is death the worst moment of their lives?

– The mystery of life and death is something no one has ever been able to reveal. We know only that no one would wish to die. Death is that moment in which men most yearn for life. It is the great portal of life, but when they approach it they are scorched by the heat. If one of the dead could awake, he would tell you what the mystery of life is. And perhaps he would ask you to explain the mystery of death in return.

– I have sometimes heard of men who returned to life after they died.

– Those struck by the sleep of a syncope. But they did not experience the supreme moment, they were halted at the threshold and felt no more than the first blast that deprived them of their senses. Only when they really died did they learn the secret of life. There was once a little courtesan who at the culminating moment of love would succumb, drowning. From her throat would come forth certain violent gurglings – *glu glu glu glu glu* – of someone dying in water, after which she would remain at the bottom for a good fifteen minutes without giving any sign of life. And then she would resurface fresher and livelier than before. Everyone wanted to try her, a try for which she charged a nice round figure. They called her the diving cocotte.

And here is Ala, the guardian of the cemetery.

Wrapped in a large fur and huddled in her armchair, the old woman doesn't take her gaze from the threshold, and she looks like a dried-out walnut in its halfshell.

– This woman has no memory of time and things; the number of her years is unknown, though some estimate it to be a thousand or more. She would have no answer for any question whatever.

– How did she manage to escape?

– As you know, Signor Perelà, death makes use of a scythe to mow the grass in her lawns, which she then carries to her barn. Well then, when she arrives here laden, she does not pause for even a moment, but throws down her bundle and rushes off to gather another. And in leaving, such is her haste that when she reaches the gate she takes a very quick step, an imperceptible skip of joy, so that her blade never touches the ground to reap this leaf of grass.

The Meadow of Love

– Signor Perelà, behold the meadow of love.

– Do all those people love one another?

– They love one another or believe they love one another. They all believe in love. Love is born from an encounter, it is a spark that ignites. Of all these paired hearts, one loves and the other lets itself be loved. The one who loves is so happy that it is sure of being loved in turn; and the power of love is such that the one who lets itself be loved is also sure of loving. A sweet deceit.

– And if each were to be in love with the other?

– When the spark ignites both parts simultaneously, it produces a conflagration that represents the most dangerous and most delusive love, the kind that is quickest to die out. If it were not so, they would go along without ever meeting, like two parallel lines.

– And if neither of the two truly loved the other?

– They would not come here, they would go directly to a cheap hotel.

– And where does their love lead them?

– Through its infinite paths which everyone travels and no one has ever succeeded in knowing.

The great round meadow is encircled by a path where magnificent chestnut trees also go in pairs, offering refreshing shade, and in the middle innumerable couples stroll. Clasped together, their interlocked hands entwining one another's waist, their heads joined, mouth against mouth, they whisper and smile at love's happiness, they gaze into each other's pupils, longing to penetrate and

116

possess one another. Neither of the two pays attention to what is happening around them, two eyes can only see two other eyes.

Maidens who idly play with rose branches, young girls barely in bloom, smile as love speaks or listen silently in rapture, and when they feel themselves pierced too deeply by their lovers' eyes they half-close their own and unwittingly inflict torture on that rose branch. Women advanced in years, almost old, stroll with a youth, almost a boy, press him with questions and drive their gaze like an Arabian dagger toward his heart. Love knows no age; age renders it stronger, tenacious, formidable. Then it is he who cannot bear it; wounded by that dagger, he lowers his head and continues along the way, absorbed in thought.

– What do they say to one another?

– They speak love's language. So intent do they seem that you would suppose that the most varied and brilliant subjects are being discussed. They have but one subject, and their repertoire may extend at the most to a few phrases, the same for all of them and always the same....Some have available to them two or three that they repeat endlessly but which seem as new as when they first spoke them; the more they repeat them, the more beautiful they sound. Or they fashion their eloquence with extremely long periods of silence interrupted by broken and infrequent words. Love has no need of words, like the great works of the creation, those works that men call mute because they cannot understand their language.

From the other side of the meadow there begins a grassy lane of brilliant green: it is lined by poplars, which cast their shadows of old men, tall, crooked, and skeletal. It is like riding on the back of a zebra.

The pairs come and go, they follow one upon the other without looking around them, and they cross one another on the scrawny shadows. It is like riding on the back of a tiger. You pass, you move on, and you walk unobserved amid the swarm of so many couples.

– Do those people think?

– Not in the least. The engine is turned off in a total abandonment, without which there is no possible happiness in love. Each one pours his own life entirely into the other, and as soon as reason intervenes love dies.

On reaching the extreme end of the lane, you turn and see it before you, long and straight, and at the other end you see a large disc that seems to have been hung there: the meadow of love.

The pairs move in a sweet, cradle-like undulation, the poplars have drawn close and have formed a covering arch, even the chestnut trees merge into one another. Everything moves in a languid torpor of vertigo, slow and even oscillations, the long shaft of the lane and the large green disc – the pendulum. The enormous pendulum that ticks off the moments for man.

– It is getting late, Signor Perelà.

– Are those people staying?

– When the sun sets, they leave; you would see them going off into the distance two by two, somewhat in a hurry and chilled, heading for the city to mingle with others. But if then you were to return when it is quite dark and you happened to go into the meadow, here and there you would hear sighs and muffled whispers.

– Some who had stayed?

– Yes.

– Even in the dark of night the pendulum swings...swings...swings...with no halt in its constant oscillation.

Iba

– Iba, Signor Perelà.

The cell receives its only light from a few rays that filter through a low grating. The iron door, which is hermetically sealed, has a glass peep-hole through which you can see the prisoner only if you remain there peering long into the darkness of the cell in an effort to discern something. Little by little there advances, as through a dissipating fog, the outline of a mass that only with great difficulty you can make out. Now there appears, in the form and color of three baked pears, an enormous, warty nose. The face is covered by a dark, shaggy fleece, and the forehead is hidden by tufts of disheveled hair that form an astonishing bush. The last thing to strike you are two points of light, two vivid rays that are never covered by lids and that dilate and contract like circles under the effect of heat.

– Five years ago, King Pelagallo died of a colic whose cause was never determined. Inquiries into a King's death are never deep, the new King interrupts the investigation, and even when the guilty one is suspected, he, more than anyone else, can live with the certainty of being the most favored of the new King's subjects. The State had no choice but to declare bankruptcy: ruin and shame. The dynasty was extinguished. To resolve the tragic situation, they resorted to an extreme expedient: "the richest citizen willing to pour out his fortune, to the very last coin, into the State's coffers will be crowned as King, whosoever he may be."

It was the morning of the contract. The most illustrious personages of the kingdom, celebrated bankers, and financiers were in the Throne Room, all bearing the inventory of their riches. Ascending the great staircase of the Royal Palace with pockets bulging, each one of them saw himself descending it with empty pockets but with a crown upon his head.

The Palace presented an unusual appearance, at once imposing and grim, as when a Sovereign's corpse lies in state. The honor guards, the escort in full uniform, and the servants in resplendent braided livery formed a hedge at the entrance as well as along the great staircase and along the sides of the Throne Room. An absolute silence reigned save for the tinkling sound of gold, so that not a single piece would be lost in the counting.

Anyone at all could become King, Signor Perelà, anyone who was ready to offer his wealth to the State in order to heal its wounds in a time when money is everything.

And lo, there comes Iba approaching the door of the Royal Palace, the very man you see in that dark cell. The city's most notorious alcoholic and brutish sot whose tongue alcohol had little by little so swollen that he could no longer speak, the butt of street urchins and the companion of all the drunkards of the most disreputable taverns, the man whom patrolmen would gather up at the break of dawn like a heap of excrement.

At first they want to bar his way, but Iba carries a large sack in each arm. And that day every citizen enjoyed the same right, just as all players are somehow the winner of the lottery before the number is drawn. He advances, tottering, but the weight of

121

the sacks serves to help him keep his legs and balance, and he even holds himself straighter than usual. As always, his thick hair is revoltingly unkempt, caked with the dirt, mire, and foul scum that he picks up in his nightly lairs which are generally the street, sheds, or the edge of a ditch. His wild beard covers his face, while his nose, a purple mushroom, seems to squirt out the blood with which it is swollen. In smiling, his two remaining teeth, the canines, seem like the props of an orangutan's distorted mouth. He is covered with dirty, threadbare rags. Up...up...he ascends the great staircase of the Royal Palace, between the rows of braided personages, the glitter of medals and sabres, the flaming color of uniforms and livery. He ascends, pausing on each step to set himself firmly on both feet before attempting the ascent to the next one.

When he reaches the Throne Room, all those present draw back suddenly with a cry of Oh!... Oh!...Oh!...prolonged, interrupted, emitted in a hundred tones and in a hundred voices, an instinctive Oh! of surprise, of disgust, of indignation, not because the man was there but because they had allowed him to enter.

A border of impeccable *redingotes* is formed; everyone has stepped aside and draws back, framing the extraordinary presence with astonishment and indignation, as though in a 'present arms!' to Iba who, there in the middle, totters, laughs... and looks around without being able to see clearly.

As soon as he is in the center of the hall, he lets the two sacks fall heavily. Everyone holds his breath. The hall is a ring of eyes that grow wide as he drops down and, with a childlike manner, unties the first of the sacks, emptying its contents onto the floor.

Pulled by the force of their popping eyes, the bystanders come forward involuntarily, and forgetting their repugnance for the filthy creature, they form a close and dense circle around Iba. The sacks are full of gold and sparkling, precious gems, neatly packed bills, and bonds from all the banks. An incredible treasure, a fabulous fortune!

What Iba let fall at the foot of the throne in order to ascend it surpassed by far that of the noblemen and the financiers of the Kingdom. And the man, stretched out on the floor in the guise of a beast, kept thrusting his hands into all that treasure, childlike, the way a boy plays with sand at the seashore; and as it was taken from him bit by bit to be inventoried, he would raise his head, laughing, himself the first to be amazed, even more so than anyone else.

Nobody could utter a word at that moment. Stretched out in the Throne Room, the gorilla laughed and laughed, revealing the two fangs that propped up the obscenity of his mouth.

How had he come by such a fortune? The vilest of beggars and most despised of men who had often stolen a few coins in order to nourish his unquenchable thirst was there with all that money. He had come to offer it to the State so as to become its Sovereign. How had he acquired it? Had he perhaps stolen it, or had he stumbled upon a treasure?

The most meticulous inquiries were made throughout the city, but no clue could be found. Nobody had been robbed, nobody had been killed. He could not be turned away. The decree was quite clear: "whosoever he may be." Nothing could be done about it, there was no way out of it. That man was to become King, and he had to be crowned.

According to law, twenty-four hours later Iba was crowned.

The Royal Palace was soon deserted. Gentlemen in waiting, dignitaries, guards and servants had all fled. Only the Royal Escort remained.

The coronation carriage awaits in the courtyard, and Iba ascends it so as to present himself in state to the people while driving through the city's main streets.

At noon sharp, amid the horses' pawing, from out of the Royal Palace comes the new King, alone, without a suite. In his right hand he raises a glass and laughs, revealing the two fangs that prop up his laughing mouth. His eyes flash ominously, and his dirty, hairy face has not been touched for the occasion. His tattered clothes are covered with dust and mire.

The coronation carriage, precious cradle of silver with magnificent gold adornments, is upholstered with purple. Drawing it are eight horses with gilded hooves and trappings. It is driven by four postillions in livery of the most solemn pomp.

Once outside, there are neither jeers nor cheers, neither shouts of insults nor cries of protest or joy. The city is deserted, not a single citizen is on the streets or at a window, the tightly shut-up houses seem to be awaiting the apocalypse.

But from a window that is cautiously opened and suddenly closed again there comes down a large bundle which breaks open on the new King's head and on his crown of jewels: shit!

After that, from all the windows and all the houses of the entire city, the same substance rains down upon him in all its varieties.

The postillions jump from the carriage to escape the precipitation which gradually turns into a downpour, and the horses begin to amble very slowly with heads lowered, as in a funeral cortège, as though the outrage is directed at them, irreparably mortifying them. The cortège continues slowly through the empty streets, unguided under the dark storm. Only the King smiles impassibly, but his smile is no longer seen because his mouth is full; his whole person drips with it, and the glass, still held high in his hand, continuously overflows with it.

Signor Perelà, it was not only ordinary men, nor was such a charge entrusted to appointed persons; indeed, the finest gentlemen of the city made a point of throwing down their own loads. And one even saw dainty white hands, in some cases elegantly gloved, thrust hastily out of the window to throw down a carefully wrapped little package of the aforesaid merchandise. From the rooftops large containers of it were emptied out, and in a short time the new King's route had become a river so turbid and dark such as no river ever was. When the cortège returned to the Palace, everyone down to the last servant had fled in horror. Iba ascended the throne and sat down. The sole evidence of this were the vestiges he left on it.

The carpet in the Throne Room, the purple upholstery of the carriage that had served for so many incoronations – everything had to be burned, and for several days the Palace was flooded with water, as was the city, in order to cleanse them of so much filth, of so much infamy. And because of the pestilential vapors, no one dared open a window for a whole week.

The King was alone in the Royal Palace while a way was being investigated to solve the intolerable situation; and the way presented itself. In the hovel where Iba used to go in order to sleep on the rare nights he was able to get there, in that remote and filthy lair were discovered two sacks of money and gems which were equal to those that the claimant had brought with him on the day of the contract. The crime did not require proceedings: 'to the very last coin' the decree read. He had defrauded the State of half of his actual wealth; the penalty was imprisonment for life.

Removed from the throne, he was questioned pro-forma and shut up in this den, the darkest cell of the whole prison-house. He had reigned four days, and his fabulous fortune remained the property of the State, which was saved by it. Thus the way was opened to the Torlindao dynasty.

How had he come by such enormous riches? In the district where he lived, an old Jew from the Levant had recently died, a banker reputed to have been extremely wealthy but who, upon his death, was found to be without a penny. Might he himself have committed his wealth to Iba? Or might it be that Iba, turning up in the house of the mysterious banker, appropriated it? Perhaps the old Jew himself aspired to be King, but, seeing death approach, took revenge for his fate by placing his whole fortune in Iba's hands. Or did he, in this way, wish to restore to the public the riches he had unlawfully acquired? There are those who assert that the

Levantine banker is a pure fantasy of the people, since such a character never existed in those parts.

Iba did not say a word; nor was it possible to interrogate him.

There, Signor Perelà, is the man who was King for four days and who saved the country from chaos and shame. Look, at his feet is a pitcher full of wine. The State supplies him with as much as he wants. The best wines from our vineyards are for him, for the captive King; it is the only boon that the State bestows upon him. A gendarme in ceremonial dress keeps guard and is replaced every two hours, day and night; it is an honor that is owed to him. Perhaps he is happy. He wallows in the excrement with which he was once crowned King.

Villa Rosa

– An absolute Monarch who has come here because of his subjects' disobedience. The Queen of Sheba is putting on all her jewels for her visit to King Solomon. Messalina is looking scornfully at the sleeping gladiator. Nero sings without any enthusiasm because Rome was long ago rebuilt. Napoleon realizes, too late, that the earth is bigger than he is. Notice how rapidly he scratches his scalp. Mary Stuart weeps for her head which has fallen into the basket, and Elizabeth of England goes wild trying to force a second-hand one on her. The Sun King is inconsolable because he is unable to see the moon. Frederick Barbarossa. One must be careful because this fellow has a penchant for biting whatever he can get at; he once bit off the ear of the man in the bed next to his. Christopher Columbus is putting his boat in a glass of water, confident that he will cross the ocean. Do you see that fellow drilling through a piece of wood? It's the Czar's head. That's a dynamiter over there, not too dangerous, however, since he creates his explosions with his mouth. And that fellow there is explaining the make-up of a new political party, but he can't find the thread.

The ecclesiastical figures, Signor Perelà. Three cardinals in a conclave. There must be a High Mass going on, listen to that uproar. Hey! Hey! Hey! Be quiet!

– Do they always quiet down like that?

– Provided one shouts loud enough. That woman is talking with Saint Catherine of Siena. Take it, go

128

ahead and take it, Signor Perelà, and be so kind as
to kneel. The Eucharist wafers are delivered fresh
to him every morning by the baker; and he keeps
them in his pyx with as much devotion as they are
kept in any other, I do believe. He is the mildest,
the most exquisitely gentle of all the inmates.
However, when passing before him, one must not
neglect this divine office. Observe the sweetness
and serenity with which he looks at you. His face
and his whole person are composed in an angelic
smile. If anyone passing by does not stop to receive
the host he holds out to him, his visage becomes
sorrowful and his eyes put forth two tears of the
most sincere and profound sadness. He doesn't
speak to anyone, and when he is spoken to, he
doesn't reply; with madness the peace of Christ has
entered into his breast.

Veronica. She wipes the faces of all, but don't
get too close, because her handkerchief is wet.
She's apt to hold it outstretched for twelve con-
secutive hours on Fridays, remaining absolutely
motionless: she seems a pillar of salt.

Saint Francis of Assisi is preaching to a turtle,
the only creature that he has succeeded in detain-
ing.

Saint Peter. He no longer has his keys, because
one day he broke a nurse's head with one of them.
Mary Magdalene and John the Baptist. Watch out,
because the pail is full of water. When he gets the
chance, he doesn't spare anyone, and it's not a
pleasant experience. We put Mary Magdalene at
his feet when she weeps too much.

Sister Crucifix. Observe the beauty of these
crosses that adorn her body: a precious collection
gathered during her youth when she was free.

– Sister Crucifix, do these crosses bring you peace or strength?

– Oh! I wear them so as to throw dust in people's eyes.

– God. The gray and white veils that he waves and incessantly wraps around himself represent clouds, and by means of this play he appears, looks around, disappears, reappears.... The fellow imagined the Divinity as an immense arbor stretched over the heads of men. From it, from its clusters of gold, descended that sweetest of liqueurs – divine clemency. One day he heard from his bishop's lips that divine wrath also exists and that God can be terrifying in his justice. His impressionable mind was left unhinged by this. He no longer saw the blessed arbor above him; rather, he saw before him a man who was just like all other men, passionate and rancorous, vengeful, with all the good and all the evil of men. Observe the Satanic flashes that dart from his eyes, with what devilish cunning he sticks two little horns onto his forehead, and the horrible shapes into which he twists his facial muscles.

And now let us pass to this other ward where the inmates are afflicted by various obsessions and are all more or less violent.

In our institution, Signor Perelà, we follow the practice of strapping patients not at the height of a fit, but as soon as the first signs of a crisis are apparent. When strapped at the height of his frenzy, the patient wastes a lot of energy. This usually happens in institutions or in wards where the inmates don't pay. Here, where everyone remits payment regularly, nothing is done to shorten their existence. Human life, even when stricken by misfortune, is sacred.

This fellow, now, claims that he is not a man, and he is convinced that all others are in error on the matter. According to him, man is something else, but he has never been able to say just what. Everyone who approaches him is met by a look of scorn mixed with pity. "Ha! You think you're a man! Well, well....Unhappy creature! Poor wretch! A man, you? Don't even think about it! Get it out of your head!" And at every change in the weather, he shouts his 'No!' furiously at one and all.

The enemy. Note especially the fixed gaze of this young man. He has the enemy within himself, and he stares at everyone with the most tragic anguish expecting to face this enemy at any moment. He knows no rest. His eyes are never closed. He stays awake and keeps watch. When he was on the outside, he would walk turning himself around for fear that his enemy might sneak up behind him.

– Does this enemy exist, or does he only imagine him?

– He may really exist; in fact, he undoubtedly exists, at least as a point of departure, or he may be the result of a misunderstanding, or he could also be wholly the fruit of his imagination. It's not an infrequent case, and, at the same time, it's one of the most agonizing states of mind known. There was a woman who had this horrible mania, though in her case the hated face so greatly feared actually existed. By some extraordinary chance that person had come into possession of a terrible secret of her life. For twenty years the woman lived in extreme anxiety, in constant terror of meeting that person. Her anguish grew in intensity with each day, and she could think only of this: "There it is, that face, I shall see it before me this very day! There! It's there looking at me and accusing me!" The face had become so engraved in her mind as to displace it and invade her whole being. Do you know where she finally met that face? In the cemetery, in one of those portraits that are placed on tombstones. The person so greatly dreaded had been dead for many years. From that moment, instead of being relieved and cured by such a discovery, the woman showed signs of mental derangement, and only then was she committed. Shortly thereafter, she died. When the tension that had filled and sustained her for twenty years suddenly fell, she lost all reason for living. A great void had grown within her.

Suicidal mania. This is the only inmate who is watched constantly. He cannot be left by himself for a moment. He is the most raving of all, and at night he sleeps strapped down. His madness is directed at himself; for the rest, he can talk with as much logic and reason as can the best organized mind, so much so that anyone would be left wondering about his real condition. He has created a philosophical system of his own according to which everything must end in suicide, and one can only agree with this system. He has tried many times to kill himself with his bare hands, ripping open his stomach or tearing at a vein: his nails have to be cut every morning. He has even tried by slamming his head on the ground, by hurling himself against the wall, or by refusing to eat and breathe. It takes three men to get a tube into him and force air and food down his throat. When he goes into the garden for his daily walk, conversing pleasantly and wittily, two strong attendants hold him by the wrists. He became insane because he was caught by the ankles just as he threw himself from a tower three hundred feet high.

– I am pleased to greet you, my dear sir; I was reading about you in our paper this very morning. You are a man of smoke, are you not?

– As you see.

– Oh! I see very well, and in these last few days I have become very interested in your case, but, with your pardon, I can approve of you only in part. Without doubt you have a great deal of merit, but how can you fail to complete your miracle? Since you were already on the fire you should have stayed there and burned to the very end. What's your point in coming back here half cooked and half raw? You are in the identical condition that I am in, and it's the worst thing that can happen to a man. That crazy father of mine grasped me by the ankles just when, as a young man, I had let myself go for the most beautiful leap in the world. Listen well to me: between me, who want to kill myself, and the others who won't let me, who is the crazier? Do you love God?

– The man I greeted a little while ago?

– No! No! That fellow is a poor idiot. Don't you know what God is? God is everything and God is nothing; for the perfection created by men cannot be anything other than nothing. They decided to give a name to nothingness, and thereby they made it become something. Like you, you are still something. Smoke is not nothing, it is smoke. By the same token, God, who is nothing, can no longer be nothing, since he is God. You could be a God for men. They need to give a body to nothingness so that nothingness can be seen and touched – at least with the imagination – so that it can be portrayed on canvas, sculpted in marble and in stone, described on paper. Thus little by little you realize that God has a nose like yours, and a handkerchief with which to blow it when he has a cold, and a mouth with which he will soon be telling you a pile of crap – anything that is to your liking or convenience – and legs to go where you yourself would like to go, ears to listen to whatever rubbish comes to your mind. And once they have turned him into a little runt like themselves, they no longer like him. Men pray to God, and do you know why? So that he may keep them as far away from himself as possible. If the devil were on earth, he would be their God. They wouldn't want any other, and they would ask to remain with him forever. They do not wish to die, ever, and they consider death the greatest calamity. Whenever they have a dead person on their hands, they begin to mourn, and there's no end to it; they never stop carrying him about on their shoulders and by all sorts of other means. They set him down and they pick him up again; they go on and on, toying with him, and they don't stop chanting until everyone has seen him. The truth is that from the time they are born they smell the stench of a corpse in their own bodies. That's why they huddle around him, pointing him out to the world in order to assure themselves and others that the terrible stench that they smell comes solely from him, belongs to him alone, and they seem to say with an air of the greatest satisfaction: "do you smell this terrible reek that befouls the air? Isn't it quite reprehensible? Well, it's not us at all. We want you to know that it's not us in any way, it's this fellow we have here on our shoulders, or here in front of us, or here behind us. He's the pig that stinks so much, he's the stinkard, he alone and nobody else!"

Men have raised a great number of towers to God, in order to get as close as possible to him, and to dupe him in the subtlest way. Those towers serve to protect them from the lightning that from time to time the Lord lets fall on their hard heads. They should be the points of departure from which to reach him, and men should leap from them at every moment – Hop! So too men soaked in alcohol or stuffed with dynamite should explode loudly in public places, in the midst of crowds at the most important gatherings, and burn, thereby setting fire everywhere: *poohm! boom! Zoohm! crack! vrrrrr...*

– Strap him, strap him. We must use precautionary measures, he may be seized by a fit. When he sees someone new he always gets excited and ends up in an awful state. Be so good as to see if His Excellency can receive Signor Perelà. Now we shall have you meet Prince Zarlino, a voluntary lunatic, an amateur-lunatic, so to speak, and, better yet, a conscious lunatic, as he says, or the lunatic twice-over, as we say. A mind constructed for lunacy, which has not found in life a pretext to justify it. He does not suffer from any obsession in particular. He is crazy for the sake of being crazy. Lunacy is his love and passion – the quintessence and sublimation of the disease. He is one of the richest men in the Realm, and at the time of the famous bankruptcy he could have become King. He sinks his wealth into this institution where he lives voluntarily; he never leaves it. He has some twenty technicians in his employ, and they second him in all his whims: a real stock company to stage any of his creations. Many of the inmates here are supported by him. He lives in their midst with a religious devotion. He is their patron and friend; he showers them with attention, kindness, and affection. He involves himself in and encourages every mania of theirs and in each one he sees a work of art that he discusses and praises; and not having any particular mania of his own, he can involve himself in and identify with all of them: he can feel crazy when and as he pleases.

– The Prince has been waiting impatiently for Signor Perelà. Show him in.

– Oh! Dear, dear, dear friend, do come forward. I am most grateful for your visit, and allow me first of all to look at you closely. For some days, now, you have aroused my interest. I have made the most meticulous inquiries concerning you, your life, and your character. I have longed for the moment when I might meet you and talk to you. Of course you must have caused amazement in everyone, I can well imagine it. Those who do not have the good fortune to live in an insane asylum and who are commonly considered to be wise are very easily astonished. A fly in the air or a falling twig is enough to make them break out into an endless series of Oh's! and Ah's! You must have noticed it. You will always hear these vowels buzzing in your ear. In here things are quite different. Here one's energy is not wasted so easily, and to arouse wonder in us takes a lot more doing. They have probably told you that I am a voluntary lunatic, an amateur-lunatic – I who hate amateurism – or the lunatic par excellence. No matter, all that doesn't interest me in the least; all that is spoken doesn't exist. Facts are what count, not words. I have already discussed your case with many inmates, seeking to make them understand the true and unique significance of your person, your real worth. I was extremely pained at not finding any minds prepared to understand you, but you may be sure that I shall succeed. One must seize the appropriate moment when dealing with such complex minds, with personalities that are so unusual and so extraordinary. And once you have entered such minds as these in the most fitting way imaginable, you may be sure that you will remain there forever. As I was saying, when we witness something that causes those on the outside to remain agape for hours, unable to articulate anything but those Ah's! and Oh's! – a clear sign of the absence of anything to say and of the emptiness in their heads – the same event is here defined by the simplest expression: an act or a gesture suffices to persuade you better than a hundred thousand words. Somebody throws a shoe or a glass at your head, and the idea enters your brain immediately and stays there forever.

All those who come to visit us have a look of sorrow, overflowing with brotherly compassion – poor people, they really are to be pitied – and at the end of their visit, we hear them pronounce with the greatest solemnity some dumb-ass thing or another, the fruit of all that weighty reflection of theirs. You can be sure that if they say dumb-ass things, it's because they are dumb-asses. Pitying our minds, which they surely take to be irreparably sick, they use words that reveal unmistakably the incurable poverty of their own. May they live untroubled; they will never go crazy. To go crazy, Signor Perelà, only one thing is required: a great, powerful, fantastic brain, whereas their brains are no larger than a flea's. So then, even if they were to go crazy their madness would be negligible, of no relevance, imperceptible, nobody would notice it, and in no way could they aspire to the honor and the joy of entering here.

Signor Perelà, I could have been King, they must have told you about that blessed bankruptcy, but I felt that after two weeks I would be a King who wanted to be anything but a King. In this miraculous place I pass my life, a supremely and wholly cerebral life that allows me to be anything and everything, and when I decide to be King I need only ring a bell and proceed to my incoronation. They all say I am mad. Fine! What do I care? That's just why I have come to live in an insane asylum. And they say it thinking to make me unhappy. They say it on purpose. Ha! Ha! Ha! Ha! It gives me my greatest satisfaction. I can go from here whenever I wish. No one can prevent me from doing so, but I wouldn't dream of spending an hour of my life outside this earthly paradise. Do take note, however... I am not crazy in the way others would have it, I am crazy in the way I wish to be and when it pleases me. This is the secret that sets me off from everyone else. The ordinary lunatic never announces what he is going to do; when the moment comes, he takes off. But I instead always announce everything I intend to do, orally or in writing, with the day's agenda compiled with meticulous, asphyxiating precision. For example, I say: at three o'clock sharp I will let out eighty-eight shrieks, shrill enough to pierce the skulls and burst the eardrums of those poor devils who must listen to them. Another lunatic would already be strapped down at the third cry. But with me, everyone is prepared to put up with my pulmonary exercise. At the eighty-eighth shriek I stop, of course, at the eighty-ninth the straight-jacket would be ready, and for reasons of public security my permission to go and come as I please would be taken away from me. That's what they're waiting for, they are all on the alert for that moment which I will never grant.

Once a week I give the papal blessing. You should see how they all prostrate themselves, and in the midst of what devotion I place the tiara on my head and don my cope: nothing like the customary indifference you find in churches on the outside where one generally goes in order to carry out a mere formality. In madmen the religious spirit is deep and highly developed. Except for sporadic and wholly personal cases in which even a sane person can arrive at an exceptional degree of spiritual intensity, it is precisely in religion that lunacy best reveals itself and thrives. As for intensity, immediately behind religious experience comes love and then, at a respectable distance, politics. Then I put on the garb of a minstrel, and playing my viola I waft sweet notes from beneath a balcony; after that the garb of a dictator. I like to strip myself naked before everyone, male and female, and I tell you in full confidence that it is not an unpleasant spectacle, since I don't have a bad build, in fact, quite the opposite. Then I'm a blacksmith, a spider, a table, a sofa... I am the moon or the sun, whatever I feel like being. One night I was a comet. Above the towers of Villa Rosa could be seen glittering my tail of silvery cloth, two hundred and fifty feet long, illuminated by powerful floodlights. I stayed up there the whole night, until the dawn caused my splendor to fade. I really did feel I was a comet, I was no longer a man, but a celestial body.

I noted everything that happened below me, in particular the reactions of the inmates. One of them shouted as though possessed that he wanted to marry me on the spot, since he was the sun. Another, because of the feeling of well-being that the sight of me instilled in him, kept repeating that the Lord had been born, and yet another, fearing that I might be too cold, tried to set fire to my tail so as to warm me up. Sensations, these, that form in my mind a living poem entitled "The Comet." Be honest with me, my dear friend, can I go out on the streets with a tail of silvery cloth two hundred and fifty feet long? Why, as soon as those wise dullards see me, they grab me, strap me and bring me here like any ordinary lunatic. No way.

Do as I say, Signor Perelà, come into this marvelous place, you too. Believe me, it's the only place where one can truly live. You'll remember me... you'll see I'm right. For an exceptional man, no other life is possible. Come now, while you still have time. What do you care about the superficial and false admiration of common people, of all those fools who on the outside are called wise and respectable? For a man like you the only admiration to be desired is that of lunatics, it's the only possible kind, since in the world, except for lunacy everything is...

Prince Zarlino shouted a filthy word, of the sort that causes our cheeks to blush and our lips to tremble when uttering it with the faintest voice in the ear of an intimate friend while doing everything possible to keep his nose from noticing it.

Delfo and Dori

– These villages, Signor Perelà, are the most charming and most picturesque of our City's surroundings. On the banks of the river they live a fraternal life, looking upon one another more with tenderness than with love. Observe the symmetry of their configuration. Two twin towers, the two churches built in the same style and adorned with the same number of statues. You would say that the roofs have an equal number of tiles and the houses an equal number of windows. The two villages live in a serene and secure peace, free of strife and peril. Between them flows the river, clear and blue, reflecting their charm and bliss. In the moonlit calm of the night from each of the two banks little boats set out, carrying young men who exchange friendly greetings in passing one another. Singing on their way and with joy in their breasts, they go to call on the maidens who are to become their brides. It is the custom for the young men of Dori to choose their wives in Delfo, and for those of Delfo in Dori.

But this exemplary peace did not always reign between them, and the river that now empties into the sea with a swell of sweetness one day brought to it the most bitter mouthful its immense gorge could swallow. This river was the scene of a most strange battle.

Know then that from that day Delfo has been inhabited by the citizens of Dori, and Dori by those of Delfo. In ancient times the two villages hated each other with that relentless and implacable hatred that characterized certain epoches, without any plausible reason and without knowing why. If you had asked them about it, they wouldn't have been able to give you an explanation. It wasn't possible to plant a bush on the bank of Delfo without a larger one, or even two, being planted in Dori. Not one stone could be removed from the one place without it falling into the other with an ominous crash.

One day a violent thunderstorm raged over the villages, and no less than eight thunderbolts fell one after the other on the little houses of Dori: eight thunderbolts and not a single victim to be mourned. Stunned by the fright but miraculously saved from death, as a sign of their boundless gratitude the poor villagers decided to raise a tower to the Virgin and to place a statue of their Divine Protectress on its top. The tower is the one you see there. No sooner had it reached the height of the houseroofs than the inquisitive eyes of Delfo spied first a certain swarming of men and then a new edifice being erected. From that moment they could no longer repress their jealousy and anger, and designs for revenge spurred all their senses.

What were they to do? Were they also to erect a tower? But they would have been left far behind in its construction, and would have finished the work with great delay. Besides, no thunderbolts had fallen on Delfo for which to thank the Virgin. And once embarked on the work, with the fear that the other might continue to build, which of the two would dare to set the final stone? Where would they set the limit? To what heights would the towers of hate and vengeance reach? Was the earth to be thrown out of balance by the construction of two new towers of Babel? They had to put a stop to it. Swift and radical action was called for. The Dorians were working like the devil to raise a tower? In Delfo, with venomous hate, work of a quite different sort was begun: boats and dinghies, rafts and shuttles, oars and poles. The river yellow with hate had never been crossed. Now was the time.

Day by day Dori grew in beauty with the erection of its superb tower, while concealed in the bosom of Delfo a monstrous creature was stirring: war.

Boats, rafts, and dinghies, shuttles, oars and poles; in a short time all was ready and the designated night arrived.

Cautiously the Delfians lowered their vessels into the river; silently and with livid faces they took their places in them.

By dint of powerful strokes, they very rapidly crossed the river and rushed into the enemy village.

The inhabitants were sleeping peacefully in the deepest of slumbers when they heard their houses being violated, their doors knocked down, their windows broken. Surprised and falling prey to confusion and terror, they fled naked from their beds, unable to defend themselves against the unexpected attack. Shouting, they fled in utter disarray, while the enemy took over their houses and settled in.

How could they have failed to anticipate the monstrous design from so treacherous, so villainous a people? How could they have failed to prepare a good defense against those murderers who lived just across the way. They fled in terror, and in their flight they all found themselves, unwittingly, on the bank of the river. Many of them had rushed there in wild despair to throw themselves into the water, others to seek safety along the bank, leaving forever.

All the houses of Dori were occupied by the enemy, and all the Dorians were away, down by the river. The river bank was crowded with boats and dinghies, with ships and shuttles. Seeing this, they understood in a flash. Driven by the force of their terror, they poured into the vessels and, rowing furiously, they shortly gained the opposite shore. Delfo was deserted; not one person had stayed behind, the houses were in perfect order, the pantries well supplied, and the beds ready to be slept in. It was a village exactly like the one they had left behind, and they settled in comfortably.

When the others on the facing shore returned triumphantly to the river in order to establish their dominion over both villages they were sure that the Dorians, having fled in panic, were far off and would make no attempt to return. But once there they no longer saw their vessels...every last one of which had crossed over to the other side. What had happened? Nothing. The two foes had conquered one another's village. The war could not have been more victorious; for the first time ever, both sides had won the same war.

They remained in this state of affairs so that neither might any longer envy the other. The boats and dinghies have since been used to maintain the good business ties and bonds of affection that have prevailed between the two villages from that day.

Hummingbird Cottage

– Signor Perelà, there also exists short-order love for those who don't have time to wait.

– Hey!

– Hee!

– Hi!

– Ho!

– Phew!

– You jolly boy, you; when you come back alone ask for me: *Mademoiselle Lilì*. You wont regret it.

At ten o'clock tomorrow morning, Signor Perelà will review the troops on the Parade Ground.

The End of Alloro

At dusk, the carriage with Perelà and his retinue was returning to the Royal Palace, where everyone was in a state of agitation over a very strange event.

Alloro, the dean of the royal servants, had disappeared the night before, and because he was in charge of the service in the King's apartments, his absence was noticed right away.

They went and looked for him in his chamber where they found his bed made up and everything in order. The old servant had not slept there. He had a daughter who lived in the city, whom he was in the habit of visiting in his free time. They hurried to her house, but she knew nothing; she hadn't seen him for three days. The poor woman became greatly alarmed and said she had a terrible feeling that her father might have committed a great folly.

The last time he had been to her house, three days earlier, he had displayed so excessive and unusual a gaiety that she was left bewildered. He seemed wrapped in a thought that made him laugh like a man possessed, and from which it was impossible to divert him. He had also seemed restless and on edge; he, usually so sedate, silent, and calm, had become a different person. He couldn't remain seated for long; he would get up and go to the window, looking out distractedly, he didn't hear what was said to him, he would lose his train of thought and begin to rub his hands together very quickly while shrugging his shoulders, beaming with hope like someone who thinks he is going to win a great prize.

They searched everywhere for him. What reason could make him hide? At mealtime he didn't appear. Could he have been seized by illness while performing some service? Where? How? When? He was already sixty years old, and such a thing was possible. Every nook and cranny was explored, but to no avail. They undertook a search in the dungeons, in the cellars, in the old armories, in the abandoned prison quarters. And now, finally, the last vault, the one that supports the corner dungeon of the Royal Palace. The vault is closed, and the door, thick and ironclad, is locked from within. But from imperceptible cracks issue acrid coils of smoke, and the pungent smell is everywhere. By means of huge pickaxes, and only with great difficulty and effort the door is dismantled and finally gives way. A thick massive cloud engulfs the onlookers, who fall back blinded. They have to wait for the smoke to thin out a little, otherwise it would be impossible to go in. But as soon as it begins to dissipate and spread out, they all rush again to the entrance. Under the large vault of the dungeon, through a dissolving cloud they begin to distinguish something. In the center a wide flattened mound of ashes and embers still burning here and there, and from the ceiling, down to about six feet from the ground, hangs a chain from which dangles a criss-cross of charred trunks slowly swaying and twisting in a horizontal position. It looks like the union of two tree trunks clumsily joined together, but it is only the remains of a human being: Alloro.

They ran to inform the King and the whole Palace. The unexpected event caused everyone to shudder with horror, and the poor Queen, who had to summon up all her strength to listen to the account, finally gave a piercing cry and fell senseless.

A few minutes later, everybody was in the dungeon, in the half-light of the torches, standing around the heap of ashes and smouldering embers, staring in horror at those human remains that swayed and twisted slowly as though to balance themselves in a horizontal position.

Was it murder? Under the royal roof and under such circumstances? More likely a suicide.

But why would the man want to end his days that way? What could have driven him to do it? Nobody was able to think of a reason. And then, how could he have thought to take his own life by choosing the most atrocious way of dying?

Everybody stood gazing, speculating, expressing their horror from time to time.

A short plump fellow, with his small hands so placed on his round belly that he seemed a tiny Buddha, gave little shudders every once in a while: "brr...brr..." as though he had a great itch and wanted to scratch his back against his clothes.

The scene in the dungeon was frightful.

The warm air and the acrid smell of smoke that brought tears to one's eyes, the ground covered with white ashes, the silence broken by whispers, and the remains of that roast suspended at eye level. With their dense and smoky flames, the torches along the walls created an ominous light and still more ominous shadows. From the ceiling hung a thick chain at whose end a man was attached by a smaller chain that clasped him under the armpits and around the chest. Because he was wholly charred, the weight of his skull perfectly balanced the rest of his body and kept it in a horizontal position, thereby causing it to revolve slowly around itself. The hands and feet no longer existed. The legs were no more than two pointed firebrands, and of the outstretched arms only stumps were left.

He must have patiently accumulated a great pile of firewood, and then, climbing up by means of a small ladder or a stool, he must have fastened himself to the chain that hung from the ceiling. Then he must have lit the fire...and stayed there waiting to be burned.

How can one make such inhuman preparations for death without faltering? How could he have not unclasped himself at the first licking of the flames? Had he been unable to free himself, or had he succeeded in exerting a superhuman will power over his flesh?

No word was found that might have justified or explained his action...nothing. The old servant had left no written word behind.

Disheveled, panting, gasping, a young woman rushes in upon the scene. They were unable to bar her way. Like a reptile she slipped out of the compassionate hands that tried to hold her back. Wild-eyed, upon reaching the dungeon door she opens her mouth wide as if to suck in all the air of the universe in one breath so that her cry may fill the whole world and reach the very heavens.

– Fool! Fool! Oh, my father, what have you done? You fool! And I who didn't understand in

time, who didn't imagine...I should have known!
You thought you could become like Perelà!

"Perelà? Perelà? Perelà?" they all shout, falling
back with a start. Nobody had thought of a
connection between Perelà and this deed. Now they
all think, deduce, make connections, letting their
imagination run freely; and each of them reconstructs the event as he sees fit: "Perelà? Perelà?
What has Perelà to do with all this?"

– Why, father? What have you done? Why have
you left me? Why did you wish to cut off both our
lives, yours and mine, in this cruel way?

"Perelà? Perelà? Perelà?" the others exclaim,
becoming more and more excited.

The woman writhes in the spasms of her sobs.

– Become...like Perelà?

– He tried to imitate Perelà?

– Nonsense!

– It's not possible!

– Why can't it be possible? It's more than possible. He too expected to become a man of smoke.

– But he's become charcoal!

– Naturally!

– Of course!

– Of smoke? Easy, easy, fellows!

– Tell us, my poor woman, how could such a
thought have entered your head?

– Ever since he came here, I mean Perelà, my
poor father was mad! Once, a few days ago, he
gave me a hint of his madness, but I didn't dream he
was capable of going this far! I couldn't understand...who could have?...He had gone wild with
admiration over that monster who has come here to
bring calamity upon us!

"Calamity? Calamity? Calamity?" everyone repeated, seized with astonishment: "Whatever are
you saying? Calamity?"

– Yes, calamity! Murderer! My father killed
himself because of him! He kept repeating; "What
did he do to become like that? How did he do it?
How did he manage it?" And one day he said to me:
"I too would like to be as he is, made of smoke."
And he would laugh and laugh; he beamed with joy
at the mere thought of it. But I thought he was
joking, I never imagined that he was serious! And I
would always answer: "And do you think that if we
burned we'd be like him?" He was crazy! He was
crazy! "If you burned," I said to him, "you'd die,
poor man, and you would also cause me to die with
grief, that's all!" Oh, father! My father!

The conjectures are many and quite varied.

Some can see no connection between Perelà and
what happened, while others see many connections
– and close ones, at that. Perelà and Alloro had
been seen together in intimate conversation, which,
to begin with, is given as a certainty. Perelà even
had him carry out errands; and Alloro, who had
soon become his man of trust, served him, radiant
with joy and with a zeal that he had never shown
even for the Sovereign himself. Might not Perelà
have instilled such a crazy notion in his head?

– If that's the case, then he's chosen the wrong
strategy for his aim – interjects one man in a sin-
gularly solemn tone.

– What? What? What? Self-incendiary propagan-
da? That's fantastic, extraordinary! – replies another
man endowed with an enormous paunch, and whose
face had turned purple because of the intense heat
and the smoke.

– An incendiary of his own self? – added caustically a very small man with the thin voice of a warbler. He had needlelike mustaches and wore gold-rimmed spectacles on a tiny nose that was so sharp-edge it looked like the blade of a knife.

– Fool! Fool!

– What an ending! – good-humoredly intervenes a handsome officer who doesn't appear to be too upset with it all.

– One lighting the way for the other!

– Just as in Nero's time, – the warbler-gentleman persists. – Just as in Nero's time! Just as in Nero's time! – And he goes on to laugh: "Hee-hee-hee..."

Another reconstructs events, suggesting that Perelà had an active part in it. Perelà could very well have fastened Alloro to the end of the chain...

– And you think the crazy old man would have let him do it?

– Or else...who knows, who knows... – says a tall, scrawny man who steps forward, bobbing a square head whose close-cropped hair begins just above the eyebrows: a perfect specimen of the true criminal. – Who knows....Who can say what happened in this den last night or this morning before dawn? Couldn't it be a case of murder?

– Murder? – At the word they all draw back in silence; and when they open their mouths again, different opinions are expressed in the most rudimentary way: "Hey! Hee! Hi! Ho! Phew!"

While the many conjectures are being set forth, the carriage with Perelà and his retinue reenters the Palace courtyard. Perelà is led to the dungeon.

– Do you see? Look at what you've done! Damn you, you old smoked toad! My father is dead!

The woman is silenced, and all those present hold their breath, staring at Perelà, studying his expression, eager to see his reaction.

He looks calmly at the carbonized man dangling from the chain, and after a minute of profound silence in that solemn emptiness he lets escape from his lips, sweetly breathed, these few words: "He wanted to become light."

The perfect calm with which the words are uttered, the sweet expression with which Perelà contemplates the scene of death, the remains of the suicide, all this exasperates and amazes those present to such an extent that they start to speak all together. The King's aide approaches Perelà in a gentle and deferential manner; and as though to invite him to reconsider, with the greatest courtesy and without any loss of composure he says:

– Become light...all well and good, my dear sir...but...it seems to me that he wanted to kill himself, doesn't it seem so to you, too? Become light...I don't believe he chose the right way. It's more than a matter of lightness...he killed himself...and in what a way...it's not the same thing.

– For goodness' sake! – squeals the warbler.

– There's something fishy here, – mutters the gentleman with the criminal face.

– If we don't get out of here, we'll all croak, – snorts the fat man whose purple face is swelling like an air balloon: "Phew!"

Perelà says nothing else. After a while the only person left in the dungeon is Alloro's daughter, mute now, dazed in her grief and with two tears, frozen at the rim of her eyelids, which cannot spill out. The soldiers on guard, the gentlemen of the

Court, the officers and servants of the Royal Palace all return upstairs to the King's apartments.

Half-spoken comments are whispered concerning Perelà's indifference. For the first time he is judged to be indifferent.

An account of what happened is quickly given to the King: Alloro's death and Perelà's indifference – an indifference that someone timidly and shudderingly dares to call cynicism. But no one ventures to express his own opinion openly, and one person hints at the opinion of another, each hoping that someone else will hurl the accusation that nobody dares be the first to hurl.

Finally, they decide to convoke the Council of State for an urgent meeting that very evening.

The military review which was to take place the next morning is postponed.

The Council of State

– I see him yet, that dear, old man with blue eyes and smiling face; there he is, serene and gentle, having reached the sixtieth year of a life of service, of honesty, of dedication. Not a shadow on his honorable person, not a spot on the mirror of his soul. The love for his King whom he served with a faithful heart; the love for his beloved daughter; the love for his God over and above everything and everyone.

The man who lived his whole life with such peace of mind, with such innocence and virtue, suddenly changes and is transformed before our eyes in a flash, his mind becomes distraught, unbalanced. His sweet and pure thoughts, previously so full of light, darken and become gloomy abysses in which lurks a mad passion, the most vertiginous folly. And after the spectacle of love and devotion that he offered us for so long, he offers us the horrendous spectacle of suicide, of a most inhuman and insane suicide, placing before our dismayed eyes a hellish scene of flames, of ashes, of smoke.

My noble sirs and most beloved brothers, I ask you, how could such a mind have gone awry so suddenly? How could the sterile tree of evil have suddenly sprouted when no evil seeds had ever been there? How, save that a fatal seed somehow did succeed in penetrating it? How could that soul have brought ruin upon itself were it not that someone, seizing upon a moment of weakness in the old man's mind, threw it into disarray and led it irreparably to the road of perdition?

– Your Eminence knows, however, that he was always a fanatical worshipper of all Kings, perhaps too much so; indeed, one could say that more than their person as such it was their supreme rank that he so fanatically loved.

– What are you suggesting by that?

– Who can assure us that that mild and humble figure did not harbor in himself, repressed until now, an unbounded ambition? An ambition disproportionate to his own person, to his own capacity, and to his own destiny?

– My dear Pipper, how can you say that? One who served his master so long and faithfully, and you call him ambitious? How, ambitious?

– He served faithfully those who in his eyes seemed great and privileged, and in his extravagant admiration he nourished, however unwittingly, a dream of power, a fruit which, unknown to all, was ripening deep in his mind. When he thought that he too could become a figure of greatness and privilege, capable, in his eyes, of feeding the vain and false admiration of the world, not even the thought of death deterred him.

– Which for all you sheep is the limit.

– Cimone, don't start in with your usual insults.

– Sheep, I said!

– Cimone, be calm for a minute.

– Nothing but a bunch of sheep!

– What we need here is calm reflection.

– We should expel him from the Grand Council, he gets more unbearable by the day.

– Not sheep? You really don't like that? Monkeys! Does that suit you? Parrots! That's still better. Not even that? Who are the most ridiculous

animals? Parrots and monkeys, you reply, decided-
ly, because they're the ones that most resemble you.

– Cimone, do us the favor of keeping quiet until
it's your turn.

– Well then, Your Eminence, what is your opinion concerning the matter?

– My opinion then...my opinion then...my
opinion is very simple, and it is just this: for some
time now in our land nothing but smoke has been
sowed, and now the land is beginning to smoke,
which seems to me only logical and quite natural. If
you sow grains of corn or wheat, you will reap ears
of corn and wheat. You have sowed smoke in abun-
dance, and now you reap an abundant harvest of
smoke; you can't expect to reap fagots of wood.
You gave excessive value to something that did not
merit it. It seemed that the world held nothing
better than smoke, it seemed that with smoke the
gravest of problems could be resolved. All we had
before our eyes was smoke: men and women were
dressed in its color; parties, balls, and banquets
were given in its honor; hymns were sung in its
praise. Honor and praise to what?

– But remember, Your Eminence, that when he
arrived you yourself rushed to pay homage to him;
no less than the rest of us, you let yourself be
deceived.

– Yes, that is true. So be it. I rushed too, but...
just a moment. In the first place, I rushed so that I
could see with my own eyes just what sort of beast
he was; and in the second place, because everybody
was rushing. It seemed as if the whole world was to
become his all at once. What do you expect....I
wished to find out for myself; and let me tell you, I
quickly realized that the beast was dangerous and

157

that it would not be long before he bit someone. And this is his bite. It has come to pass.

– And why did you not tell us right away?

– How could I have told you? Here was everybody exclaiming: "Splendid! Bravo! Wonderful! Good! What a dear!" You were ready to crown him Emperor. I too was forced to swim with the current. One mustn't stay on the outside in cases like this; nothing could be worse. One works better from the inside. This is not the time to speak up, I thought to myself; let them run as long as they want, but let us stay right behind them. As soon as they begin to get tired – people tire fast, and of everything – I'll see to whispering a few little words in their ear.

– What did he say to you in the audience you had with him, Your Eminence?

– He said...how shall I put it...the usual humbug he has always spoken, disconnected and rambling statements...that he was light...it seemed that he had no regard for anything in the world except this lightness of his....Empty-headed beliefs...heresies held by the worst kind of miscreants.

– And what would you propose we do?

– Make amends. You still have time to do it: make amends. You raised him on high? Now bring him down to his proper level, but very low, naturally, all the way down. You entrusted him with tasks of the gravest import without considering the colossal blunder you were committing? Now take those tasks back, but quickly, right away, without wasting time. And above all...remove him from society. Do as I say, find a way of making him disappear as soon as possible, without delay, and without calling people's attention to it. In cases

such as this, the less commotion the better. You
must do it very quietly, avoiding all scandal.

– Cimone, if you have anything to say, it's your
turn.

– It's a very beautiful day, really beautiful, truly
beautiful; a glorious sun shines on all things.
People are outside without their umbrellas, inanely
enjoying themselves, as they usually do: the turkeys
are strutting, the geese are waddling, the monkeys
are toddling, the parrots are jabbering, the cicadas
are chirring, the crows are cawing, the owls are
staring. Suddenly the sky turns dark, and in no time
at all there's a heavy downpour. They all run, jump,
shriek, and return to their holes. They shut themselves up in their dens, the wet crickets, the frogs,
the old moles: "eek! awk! uck!" and they get themselves good and soaked. Ha! Ha! Ha! Ha!

– My God, what an indecent man!

– The following day the storm has ended; all
that's left to be seen of it are the last empty clouds
fleeing lightly high above. All the passersby have
their umbrellas tucked under their arms, and how
they hold them tightly lest they lose them! The
baboons, the macaques, nobody is without one.
Night falls, but it hasn't rained. Ha! Ha! Ha! Ha!

– You have a curious way of laughing, as well as
of talking.

– Good Lord, what absurdities!

– He talks enigmatically because clarity would
be his ruin.

– Well then?

– What are you trying to prove with your gibes?

– That you're a pack of fools!

– And what do you think of Perelà?

– Just what I think of you, exactly the same.

– And what about yourself?

– He thinks he's so superior because he's expected to publish a book that never comes out.

– Like your Code!

– *The Day of Reckoning.*

– That's where all the greatness lies.

– In not coming out.

– The light of day might bring tears to its eyes.

– If and when it finally does come out, the mountain will have given birth to a mouse.

– Dear Cimone, your prestige lies wholly in your scorn – an easy enough thing.

– In speaking ill of everything and everyone.

– Naturally.

– And you think that that can lift you on high?

– I don't need to be lifted too high, just high enough to spit upon your heads.

– What an unreasonable man!

– By now his presence in the Grand Council is totally useless. We all know what he'll say: "Fool, or fools," according to our number.

– "Idiots..."

– "Nitwits..."

– "Simpletons..."

– "Dolts..."

– "Blockheads..."

– That's going too far.

– But come now, begging your pardon, you pass as the most learned man in the country. It doesn't do to call everyone an ass. It's unworthy of you. It's not becoming.

– And in the Grand Council.

– It's not good for the institution.

– And where do you put decorum?

– Where I put everything else.

– Why, the man's practically illiterate!

– In short, what's your opinion?

– Get out of your own stew.

– What do you think about Alloro?

– Get out of your own stew.

– What shall we do with Perelà?

– Get out of your own stew.

– A fine way to deal with problems of State.

– The whole country is waiting.

– That's what it's supposed to do.

– Di Sostegno, perhaps you should set forth your opinion.

– It seems to me that our time is being employed in the most fruitless way.

– But we've entrusted him with the Code, by God!

– We must take it back from him, by God!

– That's clear.

– But how are we to do it?

– Simple. We'll take it away from him, we'll no longer have him write it.

– But it was officially entrusted to him by Royal Decree.

– So? We'll take it back from him, officially, with another decree more royal than the first.

– And what about public opinion?

– Who gives a damn?

– And his pass?

– *Inspector General of the State...*

– *Reformer!*

– *Of men, of things, of institutions, and of customs.*

– *With full executive powers!*

– *Material, spiritual...*

– *et ultra.*

– I find that *ultra* utterly unnecessary.

– They added it as padding.

– Ha! Ha! Ha! Ha!

– What a mess!

– Ah!

– Ooh!

– We'll take it back from him and burn it, and that's that.

– Burn it at once, for God's sake!

– Hurry up and burn it! Don't leave even the smell of it behind!

– We'll return it to him in smoke!

– Just like him.

– In character.

– In his fashion.

– An excellent idea.

– And public opinion?

– Public opinion be damned!

– Who's the idiot who first mentioned the Code?

– The King!

– It was the King!

– What does the King know about it? What does the King have to do with these matters?

– He did it to take a load off his mind, don't you understand?

– He thought the man of smoke was sent to him for just this purpose – who knows from where and by whom?

– Every day he waits for messages from the other world, and that's why he doesn't get anywhere.

– He's identified himself with the role.

– He's at his wit's end.

– But the King did it so he wouldn't have to write the Code himself, it doesn't take much to see that. He thought to himself: "Who knows what

162

humbuggery will come out of it. This way, I have
nothing to do with it. Perelà's handling it, what
have I got to do with it? Let them take it up with
him. Perelà is made of smoke and is not to be
touched, he must be respected. And then even if
they touch him, they won't get much satisfaction. I
don't care a whit about them and all their codes."

– That's right.

– He jumped at the chance.

– And who's the dunce?

– We're the dunces!

– You can say that again!

– And besides, do you want to know something?

– What?

– The King isn't afraid of Perelà, because
Perelà's made of smoke. Say what you will, but
smoke will always be smoke.

– But after the Code is reformed?

– As for that...

– What do you mean by "after it's reformed"?

– Just look at what we've come to!

– What a mess we've got ourselves in!

– A real fix!

– We're at a dead-end!

– I feel completely hemmed in!

– Didn't it occur to you that in reforming the
Code that fellow could have written a first article
which declares that from now on only men of smoke
may rule and govern in our land? Didn't that occur
to you?

– Good Lord!

– It's incredible!

– It really is!

– And make himself King!

– Absolute monarch!

– We really bungled it!

– Emperor!

– My God!

– Appoint himself Czar!

– Burn all of us alive so as to turn us into men of smoke!

– Oh mother, help us!

– It's really hard to imagine just how foolish we've been.

– How lightly we behaved.

– He says he's very light, but we're even lighter.

– Why?

– Why?

– Why?

– In a way we placed in his hands the keys of our State, of our homes, of our possessions, of our family, of our children...

– Of our nieces and nephews...of our cousins...

– Of our uncles and aunts...

– Of our lives...

– All to a man of smoke!

– Just think of it!

– Without even knowing whether he's a man or not.

– In fact, he isn't.

– That's the worst of it.

– My God!

– To the first one to come along.

– What a mess!

– At least we could have waited for someone else.

– Oh sure, that's easily said: but how to find him?

– Who knows how many of them there are?

– He's probably not as unique as you think.

– They say there's a country where they come up like mushrooms.

– Who knows who he is?

– He's something without a name.

– Unbelievable!

– Incredible!

– Absurd!

– Just a moment, just a moment! Even if he had already written all the articles and amendments in the world, are we to be afraid of him?

– Smoke will always be smoke.

– With one good puff we'll send him head over heels even after he's written ten thousand codes.

– Have the wind blow him away.

– And what about public opinion?

– Public opinion be damned!

– But what if he really was sent to us?

– By whom?

– I don't know.

– We'll send him back.

– To whom?

– To whomever.

– Where?

– To Hell!

– You mean to the Devil. I get it.

– How clever you are!

– Why not?

– Then we'll send him back to the Devil!

– What if he's the Devil's shadow?

– A messenger of his?

– Why not?

– He looks just like one.

– *Mother of God!*

– The son of Satan on earth!

– Why not?

– The son of Beelzebub!

– Ooh!

– He would have to drop right in our midst!

– Precisely in this little corner of the earth!

– There's never a moment of peace.

– Didn't God once send his son? Now the Other has sent his.

– Poor us!

– We who welcomed him.

– And in such a way!

– With what honor!

– With the highest honors.

– How shameful of us!

– We really fell for it!

– I'm afraid.

– Of what?

– Of everything.

– The other one, the Son of the most high and eternal God, was persecuted and crucified.

– We gave a ball in honor of this one.

– And what a pageant!

– If he had been anything good, we would have kicked him in the behind, that's for sure.

– We never get anything right.

– That's the way it is.

– It's a trap that was set for us, you can bet on it.

– By whom?

– By somebody.

– And we fell into it.

– Headlong!

– The son of Satan!

– Absolutely!

– He's the son of Beelzebub!

– I could take an oath on it!

– The Devil's Christ!

– *Brrrr...*
– All black as he is!
– *Brrrr...*
– Actually, he's gray.
– It's all the same.
– It shouldn't have taken much to see.
– Now I see.
– Where do you expect a totally gray man to come from, if not from Hell? I'd bet my boots on it.
– And you say it so nonchalantly?
– *Brrrr...*
– *Mother of God!*
– And what if God sent this one too?
– Impossible!
– It doesn't hold!
– He sent his Son once before.
– He's not sending him again, there's no doubt about that.
– One never knows.
– He even said he would return.
– I exclude that possibility!
– Listen to me....He was fair of flesh....He was compassionate, pure, a being of light and love. This one's a thing without feelings. If he were of mud it would be all the same.
– Exactly the same.
– Precisely so.
– But after so many years...
– He may have changed color.
– Time does things like that.
– Time plays strange tricks, that's no lie.
– It doesn't hold.
– He's escaped from Hell, that's sure.

– Hear me. I am your Archbishop, and I assure you that the good Lord is as sick and tired as I am of this man of smoke!

– He was sent by the Fiend!

– My God!

– *Brrrr...*

– Poor us, we who took him into our midst!

– Your Eminence, bless us, bless us for heaven's sake! Maybe his spirit has already entered all of us!

– We must expel it!

– But how are we to do it?

– I feel it throughout my whole body!

– Let's begin at once with the exorcism.

– *In nomine Patris, et Filii, et Spiritus Sancti, Amen.*

– It would be better if he went away on his own.

– Have the wind blow him away.

– That's the second time.

– It's true, he's right. It's not very safe to pick a quarrel with the Devil.

– He too must be a rotten egg, believe me!

– For the love of God!

– We have to use tact in sending him away.

– Without letting him catch on.

– Now you're talking!

– And without letting him know that we're aware of what he really is.

– Ooh! That's not easy.

– You're always looking for complications.

– Be guided by me, I who am your Archbishop. With the help of the good Lord, we shall certainly crush him.

– And public opinion?

– We'll disclose everything!

– We'll tell what he is.

– He's committed murder!

– By God!

– And in what a way!

– Right!

– Perfect!

– We'll say that he's the son of Beelzebub, and the people will take justice into their own hands. They'll massacre him.

– Let's hand him over to the people!

– *Brrrr...*

– Yes, but first we have to tell them whose son he is.

– No! No! Let's not pick a quarrel with the Devil, I've already told you. It's not the thing to do.

– You don't want to pick a quarrel with anyone!

– Some men in this world don't have any backbone!

– Now, then, he's committed murder!

– We'll tell everything!

– There should be a trial!

– We'll hold a trial!

– Perfect!

– A trial!

– The trial!

– The trial!

– The Trial of Satan's son!

– That's right!

– I wash my hands of it!

– And I don't give a hoot about it!

– The trial of the Devil's son!

– But without saying who he is and who he isn't. It's not necessary. We shouldn't say.

– It's better to pretend that we don't know it.

– A trial as in the case of any evil-doer. We'll find a reason.

– He's committed murder!

– What a criminal!

– *Brrrr...*

– Bloody killer!

– Good!

– He wanted to burn all of us!

– Arsonist!

– Let's get on with it!

– He set a fire under the Royal Palace!

– *Brrr...*

– He wanted to burn the King!

– Regicide!

– Let's go!

– He didn't find a word to justify himself.

– How cynical!

– Ugh!

– He took advantage of a poor old man.

– How cowardly!

– Ugh!

– He must die a coward's death.

– He would have burned everybody, down to the last one of us!

– What a nice little scheme!

– He deceived public opinion.

– The most sacred thing there is!

– Sacrilegious man!

– Ugh!

– He took advantage of our trust.

– The scoundrel!

– I think things are starting to move.

– They're taking a turn for the better.

– He made fools of us!

– The monster!

– He made a fool of everyone!

– Ugh!

– He made a fool of the government!

– Despicable wretch!

– He made a fool of our Sovereign, which is worse!

– And that's going too far!

– Ugh!

– Arsonist!

– Bloody killer!

– Rotten thief!

– *Brrrr...*

– Death to him!

– Death!

– Death!

– You idiots!

– But...

– Ugh!

– Now we're getting somewhere.

Why?

The Grand Council held its meeting the very night of the day Alloro was found burned to death.

Before going up to the Council Hall, His Eminence the Archbishop went down to the dungeon where he administered absolution to the wretched remains of the old servant, and not of course as to a suicide, which is not permitted, but as to one who has been murdered. The following morning those poor remains were to be transported to the cemetery. And in fact they were transported very early and in secret. Only a few persons were in attendance, only a few learned about it. Mercifully, Alloro's daughter had been detained in the Royal Palace so that she wouldn't arouse the entire citizenry with her vociferous lamentation.

There was no wish to make a decision regarding the attitude to be assumed before the public. Was the accusation made by the Supreme Council to be let fall suddenly among the people and Perelà declared under arrest, or was it better to proceed with great caution and even more restraint, waiting first to see what turn things would take in the eyes of the public while cunningly maneuvering the affair bit by bit in the desired direction? Once the public were to cry "death!" one could go ahead with the execution in a hurry, but first one had to make sure that that little word came forth from the people's own mouth. And it wouldn't be difficult to get them to utter it, indeed, to shout it with a ringing high C. Quite the opposite, in fact.

Meanwhile, since the scene in the dungeon Perelà had not left his rooms. Nobody had come to call him, nobody had come to ask him for an explanation or to furnish him with one....Nothing. "Why?" The Council had been convened urgently, and the meeting had taken place without anyone coming to inform him or ask for his participation as they had always done in the past. "Why?"

He spent the night pondering all these things, calling to mind one by one the faces of those who were present when he arrived in the dungeon. Those faces had changed so much in his regard. The gentlemen of the Court had looked at him in a way that struck him as quite new. "Why?" Along the great staircase, when going up to the Palace apartments, they had conversed among themselves in a low voice so that he couldn't hear what they were saying, although he could tell that they were talking only of him. "Why?" What had he done? Hadn't he told the truth? Hadn't he behaved like a perfect gentleman, as he always had? Perhaps his statement had not been understood. But how could they distrust him? What did he know of what had happened? The old servant had not given him the slightest hint of what he planned to do. He would certainly have deterred him. How could he have passed on a secret of which he himself was ignorant? What did he and the old man have in common? One day Alloro had handed him the letter of the woman who was in love with him – he had been so graceful and unassuming on that occasion – and he, for his part, had simply accepted that sheet of paper without ever giving one in return. He recalled the old man's bright smile – as warm as the rays of the sun – that face which, as he looked at

him, became all red, flushed, something that radi-
ated light and heat. Poor Alloro, thought Perelà,
they probably say that he's a victim of mine,
whereas he merely wanted to become as light as I
am. But why not say something to me? Why didn't
anyone come to me last night? Why hasn't anyone
come even this morning?

Throughout the morning, in Perelà's apartment,
not a soul was seen.

The hours passed by and he didn't know what to
do. Should he go out and ask for an explanation, or
should he wait patiently? He went to the window,
looking long and intently at the sky, immersing
himself in the blue. It was a splendid day, and the
window looked out over the gardens. The sun shone
majestically over its boundless realm. The air was
rarefied, and Perelà, with his eyes half-closed, felt
himself wholly immersed, drawn into that dazzling
light.

Noon struck. He continued to wait.

The clock struck two – the hour when, on
previous days, someone would come to remind him
to go on his inspection tour. He went out and
descended to the courtyard, but the carriage that
was always waiting for him was not there. Nor
were the gentlemen who formed his retinue there.
Nothing. Nobody. "Why?"

The courtyard of the Royal Palace was unusually
deserted. Two gentlemen, were crossing the terrace
of the second floor. They were talking softly to
each other, but when they saw Perelà they withdrew
hurriedly and hid themselves behind a window in
order to spy on him. He didn't know whether he
should return and go up to his own apartment or go
out alone. He stood there for a long time,

undecided. But the light, the sun, the delicate blue attracted him to such an extent that he had to make a superhuman effort in order to remain on the ground. He crossed the Palace courtyard and was at the main gate-way in an instant. The sentinels looked at him askance and let him pass without a nod. They didn't salute him. They had always presented arms in his presence, as with the King, as with the Minister. Why then did they no longer salute him? What had happened? Why had they allowed him to go out? Why wasn't anyone speaking to him? If only he knew what to do, how to conduct himself, and what the others were doing.

He went out with this agonizing uncertainty. Very few people were about at that hour, and he was able to reach the city gates almost without being seen.

In the Royal Palace his every move had been carefully observed, and while his exit irritated some because of his apparent nonchalance, others were greatly pleased by it. He was vanishing, leaving just as he had come, perhaps never to return again. Everything would be settled without recourse to violence and without a scandal.

But there were those who wanted to carry the thorny business to the very end. They wanted justice at all costs, and instead he was being allowed to get away scot-free. The fine young fellow had got off cheap. He was leaving as though nothing had happened, after having created mayhem. It was necessary to make him pay dearly for it, detain him and punish him. Who could be sure that from afar he wouldn't be able to do the same harm or even worse? Where was he heading, anyway? To bring death to other places? That was his game. Was he

going to sow smoke in other lands? And to make
fools of other trusting men? A curious practice, to
say the least! It was necessary to put him on trial
and to give him the punishment he deserved. This is
how he should be treated, and not otherwise. Now
he was free and laughing at the simpletons he had
so easily hoodwinked from the moment he arrived.

On the other hand, there were those who claimed
that it was all to the good that he had gone off that
way, without a fuss and with his tail between his
legs – woe if we caused him to get it up! By leaving at his own pleasure, spontaneously, he wouldn't
do any further harm, whereas in defying him one
would be going up against the unknown. Who was
he? But above all, just what kind of beast was he?
Where had he come from? Where was he going?
Everyone had been satisfied with the fable he had
chosen to tell them, but nobody knew the truth
about him. He had been careful not to reveal it. An
extremely mysterious figure and so uniquely out of
the ordinary! To be rid of him in a friendly way was
a blessed miracle. This peaceful departure showed
that if Perelà was a devil – and undoubtedly he was
– he was after all a good devil, of the kind that do
harm in their spare time and only up to a point.

The whole day long, all they did was say: "he'll
come back, he'll return, you'll see, he'll come
back..."; "he won't come back, he won't return, he
won't come back again..."

But it was necessary to spread the word around,
at least in part. So in order to prepare the masses,
tell-tales were sent throughout the city: palace
servants, officials, soldiers, and gentlemen of the
Court. Some of them went to tobacco shops and let
slip half a word while selecting a cigar; others let

slip a whole word; and still others a word and a half. Some went to restaurants where, after eating and drinking, they let slip a dozen. Sipping coffee, or bowing to a lady, each divulged something, according to his social status. The people in the streets, at the doorsteps, and in the shops began to wag their tongues. The ladies of society and businessmen glued themselves to the telephone....In less than an hour, everyone knew that Perelà was suspected of complicity in Alloro's death and that even before the King ordered an inquiry he had slipped away by the dungeon door. There were some who swore that they had seen him leave by a window, and others, that when he passed by the dragoon on watch at the palace gate, the dragoon couldn't see him, since that fellow, in given circumstances, had the uncanny privilege of changing into a shadow, and in the light of the sun there was no way of seeing him. One could have quite easily come across him in the street without even noticing him.

It's not possible to relate everything that was said. We have heard of the deep impression made on the most eminent men of the State during the Supreme Assembly. We can have some idea, however faint, of what was dreamed up by women and wenches, gossips and concierges, cronies and maidservants – all creatures who are extremely impressionable by nature and who are in the habit of gathering at street-corners and doorsteps, at grocery-stores and charcuteries, at barber shops and pharmacies, at coffee-houses and cheap restaurants. "But," everyone kept repeating, "if at the Palace they consider him guilty, why let him slip away on the quiet? The guilty should be punished, dammit! Without pity and without any waste of time!"

This was quickly reported to the Royal Palace. Public opinion was taking this turn – a turn that was not at all to the liking of those up there. Moreover, they couldn't very well admit that they would rather resort to a compromise in dealing with someone supposedly in possession of occult powers which the Court, with all its footed and mounted troops and with all its retinue, didn't know how to handle. Like all men in positions of command, King Torlindao was terribly super-stitious.

Fortunately, however, without knowing the true motive for the official position, public opinion for once ended by agreeing with the Court. Yes, yes, it was better to let him go quietly. It seems that a notorious blabber had claimed to know, by way of certain close connections in the Palace, that at dawn that morning they had tried to behead Perelà, but that the blade had sliced through his neck without troubling him in the least. When those present saw him get up and walk with his head still on his shoulders they were so astounded that they lacked the wherewithal to detain him, and he went off on his merry way.

"Naturally," most people averred, "what morons not to see something so obvious! How can you chop off the head of a man of smoke? The usual foul-up of that gang: things without rhyme or reason. They never get anything right! It's much better that he's made off on his own; otherwise, with that guy in their midst they would have gone from one dumb thing to another as a matter of course, and they'd have been sure to make it worse each time. A character like that would have made monkeys of them all. They're lucky that he went away."

But at the Royal Palace this was the dilemma: "Will he come back or won't he come back? If he doesn't come back, it's better not to have him appear too guilty; but if he does come back, he must be completely eliminated, and for that the wind of public opinion must be favorable." In any case, it would be wise to be ready for the worst, now that public opinion was aroused and could be inflated or deflated at will like a sail. Wherever he may have gone, it was well to make it known that he had been dealt with severely and without indulgence. "But if he proves to be a great boon to the country he goes to," some persisted in suggesting, "they'll call us nitwits because we didn't know how to keep him, and Cimone will shout from the house-tops his inevitable word against what we've done." But by now nobody expected anything good from Perelà, and even the few who still gave him the benefit of the doubt expressed themselves with such reservations....Everyone in the Court hated him and they were resolved that the people should hate him too. And the people – who when they act as a violent mob, do not know of half-way measures – rush headlong down the path of love with a readiness that has no justification, no limit, no cause, but are just as apt to rush down the path of hatred with the very same readiness and for reasons that are no less inexplicable.

The King ordered that Alloro's daughter be free to return home. The following day an administrator would come by to settle a pension upon her, sufficient to assure her of the means to live with decorum.

And the woman was made, quite by design, to leave in full day when the whole town was busily discussing the case of Alloro and Perelà. She was made to leave the Palace on foot, and it was like throwing coals on the fire.

As soon as she was outside, all were huddling around her, asking for details, weeping and commiserating, beseeching and advising, all of them seeking to fill their lanterns with oil so that later they could illuminate their neighborhood with news and judgments.

The girl howled and wept just as she had the day before. Within a few minutes Perelà was hated as nobody had ever been hated before.

At the Royal Palace they continued to say: "Will he come back or won't he?" "My dear chap, if he comes back he'll be in a pickle."

Outside the city, Perelà had gone in the direction of the hill. He was walking along a stream, deep in thought, and he felt himself buoyed and wafted along by a luminous breeze that was gently blowing around him. He had never felt so light, and at times he thought he had lost contact with the earth and was high above it. He looked at himself, and his body no longer seemed deep gray to him but blue. He had never looked so well, and he had never imagined that he was so beautiful. His shiny boots were two enameled corollas from which his body issued like an airy flower.

He began to climb the hill, admiring the beautiful trees that stretched their strong graceful limbs toward him, limbs richly decked with green leaves

like the robe of an ancient King. He heard the tiny
stream of water babbling childlike at his feet,
insinuating itself down along the slope and darting
silver rays among the fern.

It was true, he had never seen himself so
beautiful; and he had never felt so light, never that
light. As he climbed the hill, gradually rising
above the city, his thoughts also rose higher. His
worries over the Royal Palace and its occupants
faded away in the distance, vanishing before his
gaze. Brightness vanquished everything. The
warmth of the sun and the lightness of his body, the
emerald green of the leaves and the tiny stream of
silvery water, the purity of the air he breathed,
everything made him feel that all that they were
doing down there, amidst that heap of marble and
stones, was something exceedingly heavy and
oppressive by which he felt himself overwhelmed
and crushed. The broad, massive constructions, the
very towers, and the roofs pressing down upon the
houses like helmets of lead: everything weighed
relentlessly. The Palace gentlemen dressed in
black, the soldiers clad in armor, the carriages with
their din, everything was of an oppressive and
unbearable heaviness. He stopped to observe a tree
rising high into the sky where it spread itself wide,
while on the ground its trunk occupied but a small
space, and then he turned to look down at the house
inhabited by a little man. He looked down for a
long time, there in the center, at the towers of the
Royal Palace, which a strange fate had caused to
become his home. The huge dark mass, too, reigned
over all the buildings of the city. He recalled that
first day when he had arrived there, unaware and
happy, with his spirit pure, when everything had

aroused in him one same sensation, the one he experienced now, feeling himself once more as he had been that day. Habit, the daily cares of life, and his daily distractions had dulled that impression, making things lose something of their weight, which he now experienced again with added heaviness. "I shall acquire so many fine qualities down there, but I shall lose my best quality, the only one, the true one, the one uniquely mine – this lightness that inebriates me, lifts me, and makes me happy." He thought of *Pena*, of *Rete*, of *Lama*. He scoured the whole crown of hills with his gaze, stopping on each house with the hope of recognizing which had been his, but in vain. Any number of houses in the distance might have been the one, but he couldn't be sure.

He had reached the top of the hill. About a thousand feet below, in the valley, lay the city in full panoramic view. First Perelà looked at all he could see of the sky – as much of it as the vast and distant horizon yielded to his gaze. Then he lowered his eyes again on that dark mass of stones that formed the city; and at that moment, seized by a fit of nausea, he despised it and rejected all its attraction and beauty. Once more he fixed his eyes on the sky so as to feel revived.

He was wandering on the top of the hill when he noticed a young girl sitting in the shade of an oak tree. With elbows propped on her knees, she held her face between her hands. She was staring fixedly, as in a trance, at the panorama of the city. A stick lay across her lap, and some twenty sheep were dozing around her. When Perelà was near her, the startled girl jumped up with a cry and skipped back a few steps, letting the staff fall and clasping her frightened face even more firmly between her hands.

– Oh!

– Are you afraid? – asked Perelà, smiling. – Are you afraid of me?

– Forgive me, sir, for a moment I took you for a ghost....But if you don't frighten me, I won't be scared.

Perelà looked at her so sweetly that the girl approached him, calm and reassured.

– What were you looking at so intently?

– I was looking at the city. When the sheep doze in the afternoon, I enjoy myself by looking at the city. It's the only pleasure I have. Have you just come from there?

– Yes.

– I've never had a chance to go there. I always go out in the company of my sheep, and I can't leave them. I'd be in trouble. Sometimes I feel a wild desire to leave them on their own and run away down there. But then...barefoot...dressed this way...what would they say of me? Perhaps they wouldn't let me in. My cruel mistress doesn't give me a single day off a year, and I'm dying to see the city. But do tell me, sir, are you perhaps made of smoke?

– Yes.

– A few days ago my mistress and her friends were saying that in the city there are all sorts of beautiful things – things that can be seen only down there – there was even a man of smoke who made everyone marvel, but I thought she was joking. Would you be the one?

– Yes.

The little girl became speechless, as though she didn't dare to look at Perelà after his assertion, but then, fearful of keeping silent in his presence, she began to talk aloud to herself.

– The four towers in the middle down there belong to the King, and the building you see all around them is his house. The dome and the belfry belong to the church, which is called the Cathedral. That building that comes to a point, with the white statues in the front, is the theater, where the great ladies go in the evening half-naked and covered only with flowers and gems so they can show themselves to their lovers. The glitter that dazzles your eyes are the carriages that take them riding around. The huge house that's all black without windows is the convent where the penitents – those women who sinned too much – are confined. Inside there they weep so that the Lord may forget their sins. In that house that's all pink the poor lunatics are confined.

– Tell me, my child, do you always look down below toward the earth, and do you never raise your eyes up to the sky?

– Oh! I see so much of the sky, if you only knew, and I've seen so much of it that I won't lift up my head again to look at it. The sky is always the same and it's all the same. I want to look where I've never looked before. The sky is something you look at at night when the stars are shining; but I want to get to know the other stars of the night, those that shine in the Palace halls or in the theater, half-naked for their lovers.

The sun was setting, and after bidding farewell to the girl who was still looking down below toward the earth, Perelà looked up once again at the sky and then began to descend rapidly to the city. When he arrived there, the sun had just set and dark was beginning to fall.

At the gate the toll officers looked at him suspiciously from head to toe, without any show of respect, and as he passed by they cast some snide remarks at him, which he failed to grasp. The first person he met was a woman who when she was near him cried out "phew!" and moved away from him as though she was afraid of catching the plague. Then everybody rushed to their doorways and windows; and as he went by they assailed him with insults, vulgar gestures, obscene words, and shouts of contempt and scorn.

A small boy standing in the middle of the street came up to him and gave him a push that Perelà was unable to withstand. Tottering in his boots, he finally crashed into the wall. Beaming with instinctive cruelty at his success, the tyke came up to him again and with a still stronger push sent him reeling to the other side of the street. A second boy rushed up to help his friend in the exploit, and together they began to toss him back and forth without his being able to put up any resistance. Once his weakness was discovered, a third and then a fourth boy joined in to make sport of him – an inflated balloon that they toyed with, shouting and laughing all the while. Soon there was a horde of them, one nastier than the other, one more ruthless than the other in their successful game. In the middle of them, humiliated, irreparably disheartened, racked with pain, without a way of defending himself against the merciless swarm, Perelà felt himself swept away by all that shoving, while the laughter and joyful shouts pierced his heart. From the windows, from the doorsteps, nobody railed at him, but everyone exulted obscenely, bursting their sides with laughter in approval. And the horde of boys increased in number. Egged on and spurred by the grown-ups, they threw themselves with added fervor into their newly invented sport. Perelà looked toward the grown-ups while he was being tossed about by the youngsters, and his supplicating look said: "Why?" Why did no one rush to defend him, to deliver him from those tiny hands that had become as cruel as those of the fiercest enemy? Now they were hurling him to the ground and picking him up, all of them exploding with laughter. No one intervened to impose respect for the delicate, exceptional constitution with which he had been privileged. Rather, everyone made way for the gang of children so that they would be free to carry out their feat to the very end. He was pilloried, and what a horrible pillorying, the most humiliating that ever befell a man! In the midst of a swarm of little curlyheads, silver peals, trebling voices and cherubic laughter, he could do nothing to defend himself. One of them – no more than three years old, beautiful beyond words, and with a long twig clenched like a cigar between his little teeth – laughed and laughed while approaching with the most innocent gaiety in order to give a shove. But he himself was being bumped, bowled over and dumped to the ground, all of which pleased him no end. He would get up again as though he were made of rubber and prepare to give a new shove, laughing more and more while clenching the twig between his little teeth.

Those little curlytops had unwittingly found the most excruciating way to humiliate a man. From the doorsteps and the windows, the grown-ups merely went on laughing obscenely, and whenever the ferocity of the insects reached a frenzied pitch, they would shout "Bravo! Well done! Keep it up! Go to it!" so as to further incite them. Foundering, lost, and powerless because of his extreme lightness to defend himself against a swarm of children, there in the middle of the street Perelà had become the butt of all. And the pained expression of his poor face continued to ask: "Why? Why?"

Perelà's Indisposition

Perelà is confined to his quarters, indisposed.

The Court physician has come to visit him, but declares that he doesn't know what to do. Asserting that he was unable to locate the patient's heart and pulse, he has ended by refusing to give his attention to a man of smoke and has pronounced the indisposition to be an outright sham, a mere pretext. Coming out of the bedroom he had shrugged his shoulders, without deigning to bid farewell to the patient.

It is not a sham, it is not a pretext. Perelà really does feel ill.

After the scene in the street, having escaped only when the urchins had tired of their game, he reentered the Royal Palace feeling utterly worn out and shattered. He couldn't say exactly where he was in pain, but his fragile limbs seemed rent. His beautiful gray eyes still had tears in them, he felt dizzy, and from time to time he was seized by shivers that shook him violently. His boots had become cold to the touch of his legs, and it was ice-cold all around him. He was assailed by an extreme need to warm himself, but because it was already spring there could be no lit stove, nor would he have dared ask for one.

Nobody came to visit him except the physician who, after a few minutes, left in such a rude manner.

"What is happening?" he thinks to himself: "Oh! if only I hadn't returned. Yesterday afternoon I was happy up there, and I already felt I was close to the sky. Why did I return? What is it about this earth that draws me into the cold of its valleys, into the darkness of its turbid inlets? Oh! the beautiful hill, and the blue that I felt was mine! What do these people want with me? What will they do to me? They are plotting something against me, I feel it. What did I do to them? If only old Alloro were here! He's dead...dead! They probably say that he died because of me, that I am the cause of his death. He's dead...he who would have been the only one to take pity on me. He would have come secretly to inform me concerning my fate, to tell me what they intend to do to me and what they're plotting behind my back. Everything has been overturned before my eyes in an instant..."

While Perelà is absorbed in these thoughts, the door of the room is cautiously opened, and like a cloud, swishing with silk and veils, a woman enters – the Marchesa Oliva di Bellonda.

– They didn't want to let me in. I had to struggle bodily with the dragoon...he threatened to run me through with his bayonet, to fire upon me. I invoked the help of the King, my cousin, in vain; of ministers and gentlemen of the Court, in vain. Nothing from anyone, no, nothing! Scoundrels! Cowards! Only from a woman was I able to obtain assistance, a woman who knows and understands – the Queen, through her grace alone. She knows what suffering is. I don't know how she did it; perhaps she implored on my behalf and got them to let me pass. I have come only to tell you that I love you, that I still love you, and that I shall love you unto eternity. When I heard about it, when yesterday they were telling me of that revolting scene...I was momentarily annihilated. I should have rushed there to save you! Looking at my own children, I felt a flush of anger, but then I realized that only the grown-ups are truly responsible. Children do not yet know how cruel they too can be. If only I could have rushed there to help you, to free you!

Dear friend...I do not know what will become of you...I believe that the Council of those vile men is meeting at this very moment in order to decide your fate. Who knows what decision will be taken? But they are certain to want a victim, two, three if possible – their thirst is insatiable! They will want to do you harm, of this I am sure! I will fight, I will do everything to save you, I will consider all means to be legitimate. Nothing shall remain impossible and untried in my efforts to aid you to the end! And after they have crushed you, if indeed they succeed in doing so, I shall wish only to perish with you, and I will be content, happy – it shall be my goal, my conquest, my victory! But I tremble...for this alone I tremble – that you should fall without me! If you are lost, I too must be lost; I must follow you wheresoever, and I must die with you if you die! Only thus will I be saved, this is my hour! I will use all means: the sharpest blades to pierce their hearts while I laugh; with all the wiles, with all the lies, with all the vileness I have learned from them, I shall draw them into my nets, body and soul; with a smile born of my hatred, I shall burn everything; I shall poison, I shall destroy, until they let me die with you! *Pena! Rete! Lama!* Give unto my pitiless hands the instruments of destruction and the might of vengeance! I do not know what will happen, but remember that I am always at your side. Farewell...farewell...my great love!

The Marchesa Oliva di Bellonda having disappeared like a shadow, Perelà reflects upon this woman's love and upon her sacrifice. The one creature who has loved him. He thinks of her and of Alloro. Perhaps she too will be burned by her love, as the old servant was by his devotion.... "But then they are right to hate me, if to love me means to succumb. They are right. They are obeying their animal instinct to survive. Why did Alloro kill himself? Why does this woman wish to die? And yet I said nothing to them; I did not even lead them to suppose that I returned their friendship and their affection."

At this point the door opens and the gentleman with the square head and gold-rimmed spectacles appears. From behind him two heads swollen with curiosity crane forward to look into the room.

– Signor Perelà, you are ordered to appear at ten o'clock tomorrow morning before the Minister of Justice. Come prepared with your defense and your lawyers.

The Trial of Perelà

The courtroom in the Palace of Justice is crowded. For some minutes Perelà has been in the prisoner's dock, surrounded by twelve guards in full uniform.

His entrance was greeted with furious cries of derision, hooting, gibes, obscenities.

Only after several minutes was it possible to reestablish order and silence.

His countenance is the same as it always has been, not changed in the least. He shows little interest in what is happening around him.

The galleries are overflowing; elegant ladies and damsels are crowded together there. There is a great stirring of feathers, lorgnettes, and fans. One sees men and women of all ages.

Behind the banister a horde of people pack the courtroom all the way back beyond the open doors.

Already at seven o'clock in the morning the avenue and the environs of the Palace of Justice were crammed with people.

When Perelà's carriage went by, the shouting and hooting broke out into a hellish storm.

It is ten o'clock.

Everyone is waiting for the Minister of Justice who will be accompanied by the judges.

All eyes are turned toward the accused. From the sea of people at the back of the courtroom, heads are continually bobbing up and down in an attempt to get a glimpse of the man. That rising and falling of heads creates the impression of a storm in an ocean of potatoes.

Throughout the courtroom there is shouting and whispering, but it is impossible to make out a single word.

The air one breathes is dank and steamy, a horrible blend of decaying wood and decaying upholstery, ancient grease and recent exhalations of young and old humanity. With all their irony some spirals of Coty and Houbigant perfumes manage to infiltrate the air, only to dissipate after a short while, similar to certain mischievous feminine smiles – as sharp as a razor's edge. The whole is a blend made up of and perfected by the very mixture of the crowd itself, the blend that is typical of certain large public theaters, political and academic halls, reaching its highest expression in the halls of Justice on the day of a great trial.

As though by magic, a sepulchral silence falls. The green door-curtains with long fringes are opened and the Minister of Justice enters, followed by his retinue. In the courtroom, which suddenly seems empty, you hear only the rumbling of massive armchairs being moved on the boards of the floor – like thunder that announces the storm.

The Minister of Justice remains standing, and in the absolute stillness of the room he looks all around.

Only Perelà sways a little, as though trying to find the position that will keep him fixed on the ground.

The Minister begins to speak.

– Before the trial starts...who is the defense lawyer for the accused?

Silence.

The Minister fixes his gaze on Perelà.

Imperceptibly, Perelà sways again.
– You, the accused, who is your lawyer?
Silence.
One can sense some cracking in the compactness
of the whole.
– Have you no lawyer? You have the right to be
defended.
The whole creaks, continuing its cracking with
some noise.
– Well, then, who wants to defend him?
The cracks widen noisily.
– Will no one answer?
Some of the cracks become chasms, and the first
pieces start falling with a crash.
– Is there nobody who will defend him?
Now it is a general rolling of ever bigger
boulders which rumble down and break into pieces.
– Would not this proof and your silence suffice
to declare your guilt?
Everything is collapsing, coming apart, crum-
bling; the place is in smithereens.
– Silence!
– For the last time: Is there anybody here who
wants to speak in defense of the accused?
– I do.
– A woman?
– Oliva!
– Oliva!
– The Marchesa di Bellonda.
– She's crazy!
– Women are not allowed to have such a func-
tion! Our laws do not permit it.
– Get the women out of here!
– Women have never defended anyone!

Some shout while others laugh, some sneeze and blow their noses, others rail and make an uproar. On the bench, bells are ringing – one of them is cracked. The call for silence results in more noise than ever. The cracked bell belongs to the Minister of Justice.

– Madam, the word of a woman has never had any weight in the halls of Justice.
– Signor Perelà has the right to be defended.
– But not by a woman.
– Since the generosity of men can find no word on his behalf, let at least the word of a woman be heard.
– This trial is taking a rather bad turn.

– The charge!
– Silence!
– Silence in the Court!
All the bells are dancing the can-can.
The cracked bell sounds like an elderly feminist baroness engaged in a discussion with her fervid admirers – all between fifteen and twenty years old.
– The charge!
– Accused, you stand charged with having availed yourself of fiendish arts in order to deceive the King, the Council of Ministers, and public opinion. By virtue of your peculiar nature you created the belief that you were capable of performing a high mission for our land, when in fact you were fully aware of your absolute impotence and your total insignificance. And you did so in order to carry out your criminal intent which is now discovered.

You have, until the very last, kept the office generously bestowed upon you instead of honestly surrendering it.

You are further charged with using the afore-mentioned fiendish arts in order to induce a man to commit suicide. Alloro is your first victim. In keeping with your plan, you would have continued an effective and well-orchestrated campaign of incendiary and homicidal carnage, burning people and things so as to be left the terrible and absolute master of the field. You are accused of entering our land with the express aim of doing injury, relying on your mysterious and illicit power. Defend yourself.

A relative quiet ensues.

Throughout the courtroom there are people hushing. They want to hear Perelà's defense. The bells have their skirts lowered.

And as soon as Perelà begins to move, to sway a little, making as to speak, a total silence falls over the courtroom.

– I am light. – He pronounces these words distinctly yet softly, his voice steady and calm, with all the gentleness of his usual expression and an angelic sweetness.

– Well, then! Defend yourself!

– I am light, – he replies in an even sweeter tone.

The courtroom rumbles again; cries of strong indignation are raised.

– And with that declaration is it perhaps your aim to hurl at us your final insult? Are you trying to make fools of us yet again with your malevolent and reprehensible irony, with your wretched cynicism? Are you suggesting that we entrusted to the lightest of men the weightiest of tasks, is that what you mean? Well, we have relieved that man of the task, and now we shall give him the punishment he deserves. The mysterious power of your person has been uncovered; aha! you are the child...of three witches!

   – No! No! No! *Pena! Rete! Lama!* Look upon me. You see where I am. Come forth from the grave! Tell me you were not three witches!

This dramatic moment scandalizes many faces, which begin to contort, but here and there white handkerchiefs are seen unfolding.

   – Signor Perelà, for the last time, defend yourself!

   – I am very light, yes, yes, so-o-o light, extremely light.

   – It seems rather that you're getting a bit heavy.

   – Why should he defend himself? He feels great being guilty!

   – He's waiting with resignation to be sentenced!

   – Silence!

   – Have you nothing else to say? Let us proceed to the interrogation of the witnesses.

There is a moment of heated debate, of minor rows and squabbles, gestures, greetings, smiles. Everyone is in a flurry except for a woman who with head bowed stands in the center, not far from the magistrate's bench: the Marchesa Oliva di Bellonda.

   – Francesco Maria Parlottini, Archbishop.

   – Have you ever had any relations with the accused?

   – Brief but more than enough.

   – What did you take him to be?

– A being noxious to Church and State: to the State of the Church and to the Church of the State.

– Do you believe that he availed himself of fiendish arts in order to deceive the King, the Council of Ministers, and public opinion?

– He availed himself of fiendish theories, most pernicious ones, which is much worse.

– Do you hold him responsible for Alloro's death?

– Directly so.

– Do you believe he would have continued his incendiary and homicidal campaign?

– Without doubt.

– What would you do with him?

– Inasmuch as beheading is highly problematical in this case, and hanging no less so – a fact that renders both the axe and the noose somewhat unreliable – and since the accused is on the most intimate terms with fire, of which, being its inseparable companion, he surely enjoys the highest favors, I would see whether a trial by water, carefully devised, would be to his liking.

– Teodoro Di Sostegno, banker.

– Have you ever had any relations with the accused?

– Yes.

– What did you take him to be?

– An object of curiosity, nothing more and nothing less.

– Do you believe that he availed himself of fiendish arts so as to deceive, etc.?...

– Incontestably, for the sake of mere curiosity.

– Do you hold him responsible for Alloro's death?

– An initial experiment out of pure curiosity.

– Do you believe he would have continued his incendiary campaign, etc.?...

– Most assuredly, so as to attract the whole world's curiosity.

– What would you do with him?

– Put him up at a public auction for the connoisseurs of the genre. I guarantee its success.

– Angiolino Dal Soffio, poet.

– Have you ever had any relations with the accused?

– Yes.

– What did you take him to be?

– A man who is all feet.

– Do you believe he availed himself of fiendish arts?...

– Pedestrian arts.

– Do you hold him responsible for Alloro's death?

– The author of it.

– Do you believe he would have continued his incendiary campaign, etc.?...

– As a co-author.

– What would you do with him?

– I would send him with compliments to my critic Cristoforo Soffiato who would rake him over the coals if he could find a way.

– Cristoforo Soffiato, critic.

– Have you ever had any relations with the accused?

– I have...and I haven't.

– Did you or didn't you?

– I did.

– What did you take him to be?

– I took him to be...and I didn't take him to be...

– Do you believe he availed himself of fiendish arts, etc.?...

– He did...and he didn't.

– Did he or didn't he?

– He did.

– Do you hold him responsible for Alloro's death?

– I do...and I don't.

– What would you do with him?

– I would...

– And you wouldn't.

– Cesare Augusto Bellezza, sculptor.

– Have you ever had any relations with the accused?

– Yes.

– What did you take him to be?

– A poltroon, nothing more and nothing less.

– But you began work on a monument to him.

– Yes.

– Can you explain why?

– I have made monuments to all heroes.

– And now you are starting on monuments for poltroons?

– So that the splendor of the former can shine the brighter by comparison with the latter.

– Do you believe he availed himself of fiendish arts, etc.?...

– Diabolic arts.

– Do you hold him responsible for Alloro's death?

– As much as Satan himself.

– Do you believe he would have continued his incendiary campaign, etc.?...

– As though Lucifer had returned to the earth.

– What would you do with him?

– I would bind him as Prometheus was bound and throw him into the wash-tub to be bleached.

– Gastone Speranza, painter.

– Have you ever had any relations with the accused?

– Yes.

– What did you take him to be?

– A colorless man with crafty designs.

– Do you believe he availed himself of fiendish arts, etc.?...

– Extremely dark arts, almost black.

– Do you hold him responsible for Alloro's death?

– Indeed, with one stroke.

– Do you believe he would have continued his incendiary campaign, etc.?...

– Yes, but all out of perspective.

– What would you do with him?

– I would try to make him become red.

– Sebastiano Pipper, physician.

– Have you ever had any relations with the accused?

– I had occasion to see him.

– What did you take him to be?

– Someone afflicted with *psychopoloneuropatho-schlerosophilia*.

– Is it contagious?

– Ooh! an extremely contagious disease!

– And only now you tell us?

– Unfortunately!

– Do you believe he availed himself of fiendish arts, etc.?...

– Infected arts.

– Do you hold him responsible for Alloro's death?

– He infected him directly and right to the marrow.

– Do you believe he would have continued his incendiary campaign, etc.?...

– To the point of causing an epidemic.

– What would you do with him?

– I would put him in quicklime, and without a moment's delay.

– Cima Guscio, philosopher, known as Cimone.

– Have you ever had any relations with the accused?

– Yes.

– What did you take him to be?

– An imbecile.

– Do you believe he availed himself of fiendish arts, etc.?...

– Yes, but expressly to deceive imbeciles, and he succeeded in it perfectly.

– Do you hold him responsible for Alloro's death?

– One was more of an imbecile than the other.

– Do you believe he would have continued his incendiary campaign, etc.?...

– Yes, but among imbeciles, who are numberless.

– What would you do with him?

– One imbecile more or one imbecile less...

– You too, you too, vile and perverse philosopher, you who are on earth to reveal its gangrene;

deliver us at least from yours which is the foulest of
all!
 – Marchesa, it is not your turn.
 – Make her be quiet!
 – She must keep silent!
 – This trial is like a *pochade!*
 – It's a perfect farce!

 – Zoë Bolo Filzo.
 – Have you ever had any relations with the
accused?
 – I believe so.
 – What did you take him to be?
 – A monster.
 – Do you believe he availed himself of fiendish
arts, etc.?...
 – Monstrous arts.
 – Do you hold him responsible for Alloro's
death?
 – Absolutely so.
 – Do you believe he would have continued his
incendiary campaign, etc.?...
 – With zeal.
 – What would you do with him?
 – Make a gift of him to the museum of mummies.

 – Maria Gioconda di Cartella.
 – Have you ever had any relations with the
accused?
 – Yes.
 – What did you take him to be?
 – One who is impotent in the cause of good and
very potent in the cause of evil.
 – Do you believe he availed himself of fiendish
arts, etc.?...

– Of the most abominable kind.
– Do you hold him responsible for Alloro's death?
– Without question.
– Do you believe he would have continued his incendiary campaign, etc.?...
– Without respite.
– What would you do with him?
– I would try frying him.

– Chloe Pizzardini Ba.
– Have you ever had any relations with the accused?
– Nothing to speak of.
– And what did you take him to be?
– A good-for-nothing.
– Do you believe he availed himself of fiendish arts, etc.?...
– Arts worth nothing.
– Do you hold him responsible for Alloro's death?
– They were two non-entities.
– Do you believe he would have continued his incendiary campaign, etc.?...
– As though it were nothing at all.
– What would you do with him?
– I? Why, nothing, nothing whatsoever.

– Nadia Giunchi del Bacchetto.
– Have you ever had relations with the accused?
– No.
– Well then, dear lady, it's needless to continue your interrogation.
– At least you can ask me what I would like to do with him.

– What would you do with him?

– I would stuff him into the eyes, up the noses and down the throats of my dear friends.

– How vulgar she is!

– She just wanted to show off in the middle of the trial!

– In front of all the riff-raff here.

– If they take aim at us, we'll be in a fine fix!

– Bianca Delfino Bicco Delle Catene.

– Have you ever had any relations with the accused?

– Yes, one day, from a distance.

– And on that distant day what did you take him to be?

– A corpse...just come forth from the tomb.

– Do you believe he availed himself of fiendish arts, etc.?...

– Of all those arts that lead to death.

– Do you hold him responsible for Alloro's death?

– Death is his kingdom.

– Do you believe he would have continued his incendiary campaign, etc.?...

– To the point of turning the earth into a graveyard.

– What would you do with him?

– I would give him a new grave in my cemetery.

– Enos Copertino. Be it known that though clothed in trousers and bearing a masculine name, with respect to the law the witness remains of the female sex.

– *Et voilà la lesbienne!*

– *Avec sa jupe-culotte!*

– Have you ever had any relations with the accused?

– *Bien peu, monsieur.*

– What did you take him to be?

– *Un voyeur.*

– *Mon Dieu, quelle honte!*

– *C'est le dernier outrage.*

– Do you believe he availed himself of fiendish arts, etc.?...

– *Certainement.*

– Do you hold him responsible for Alloro's death?

– *Il était son type.*

– *Ah! La vielle tante!*

– *Quelle horrible créature!*

– *C'est une chose affreuse.*

– *Il me dégoute.*

– What would you do with him?

– *Je m'en fous.*

– Rosalinda Panciera, widow Bonsemblant.

– Have you ever had any relations with the accused?

– Yes, but from a respectable distance.

– What did you take him to be from such a distance?

– Somebody not in the least worth getting close to.

– Do you believe he availed himself of fiendish arts, etc.?...

– The most useless of all arts.

– Do you hold him responsible for Alloro's death?

– The most useless of murderers.

– What would you do with him?

– I would place him among useless things, in the attic.

– Carmen Ilario Denza.
– Have you ever had any relations with the accused?
– Yes.
– What did you take him to be?
– A cheap exploiter of women.
– Do you believe he availed himself of fiendish arts, etc.?...
– The vulgar arts of a pimp.
– Do you hold him responsible for Alloro's death?
– His murderer.
– Do you believe he would have continued his incendiary campaign, etc.?...
– Without compunction.
– What would you do with him?
– Something that would finish him as a topic of conversation.

– Rosa Ramino Liccio.
– Have you ever had any relations with the accused?
– Yes.
– What did you take him to be?
– A shameless sort.
– Do you believe he availed himself of fiendish arts, etc.?...
– Arts of shamelessness.
– Do you hold him responsible for Alloro's death?
– He caused him to die of shame.
– What would you do with him?

207

– Since he has only his boots to take off, he's not for me.

– Gelasia Del Prado Soliès.
– Have you ever had any relations with the accused?
– Alas, yes.
– What did you take him to be?
– The most boring man in the world.
– Do you believe he availed himself of fiendish arts, etc.?...
– He made use of boredom, which is the worst disease in the world.
– Do you hold him responsible for Alloro's death?
– He infected him with his own disease.
– Do you believe he would have continued his incendiary campaign, etc.?...
– To the point of causing all of us to die of boredom.
– What would you do with him?
– He has bored me so much that I'm unable to say.

– The witness Giacomina Barbero di Ca' Mucchio, incapable of testifying, has had her medical certificate sent to us.
– Lady Giacomina is missing!
– It's true. I hadn't noticed.
– "Giacomina Barbero di Ca' Mucchio – Silence! – examined by me, is suffering from severe bruises and multiple abrasions of the vagina, with ensuing inflammation of the area: prognosis highly uncertain. As a result she is absolutely incapable of moving and walking to testify in criminal trials. By

this signature, I affirm the above to be true.
Pipper."
– Charles-Mini?
– He's ruined her!
– Is it possible that this late in life he's contin-
uing his natural growth?
– No. She must have made a try with Charles-le
Grand.

– Marchesa Oliva di Bellonda, what do you wish
to say?
– Just one word. After all that has been said, just
one word is left to me: I am light...yes...I am light,
so very very light, extremely light.
She raises her arms high, fluttering the gray veils
that wrap her body and makes as if to fly.
Like a cyclone, shouts and hoots are let loose on
all sides. A bugle blast is also heard. Impassive,
the Marchesa Oliva di Bellonda waits.
– Lock her up too in the prisoner's cage!
– Along with her pig of a lover!
– Tie them together!
– Madwoman!
– Jezebel!
– Spank her in public in the presence of that
stinking Perelà!
The Marchesa raises an arm while keeping her
head bowed. A semblance of silence returns.
    – Curse...insult...swear...since that is all you
can do! It's only right that you do so, because you
hurl yourselves only against great things. – There
are shouts, hoots, swearing. – You could do nothing
better to betray yourselves. Paltry, miserable
wretches generated in bloody, viscous wombs by
virtue of carnal lust, you who have issued forth like

reptiles amidst the writhing of muscles and the
frenzy of bowels. He is above all lineage and
above all blood! He is the son of the fertile old age
of three virgins who nursed him not with the loathsome fluid of their bosoms, but with the enchantment of poetry in their voices, with the warmth of
the flame in their hearts. Blindly you praised
Fortune who sent him to you, and with the same
blindness you execrate her. You are so base that you
can resort only to lies and insults... – There are
shouts, hoots, obscene words and other noises: the
bugles are now more than one. – You are preparing
for this man the same punishment you give to
thieves and murderers. But he was new among you;
try to be new with him if you can! – Shouts, hoots,
all sorts of noises; the bugles have expanded into
an orchestra. The Marchesa shouts at the top of her
lungs, but only those closest to her can hear what
she says. – Is not Alloro's end clear proof of this
man's exceptional power? And were he, in his
charisma, to burn everything and everyone in a
sublime aspiration to heaven, would he not be the
greatest, the most infinitely great of all men?

– She's mad!

– Make her keep quiet!

– She's a woman!

– She's in love!

– She needs to be spanked in front of everyone!

– Burn her too, seeing that she's so fond of
smoke!

The noise gets louder and becomes a confused
hubbub. Only some insults can be understood from
time to time – the worst ones. There is a great
cancan of bells on the Minister's bench.

– Silence!

– Surly-faced men green with the poison of your invectives, look upon him! There he stands, serene, tranquil, unchanged! What has he said to exonerate himself? "I am light." And with him and like him, I feel light; and with laughter I defy the wrath of all! Oh! You do not frighten me, wretched people, I defy all of you, from first to last, you who are so many against me alone!

Again she raises her arms high, fluttering the gray veils around her as though she were flying. Oliva di Bellonda was never so beautiful.

– Make her shut up once and for all!

– They should stop her mouth up!

– They should stop up everything in her!

– They can't even get a woman to keep quiet.

– Well, that's the hardest thing in the world to do.

– Look at me! Look at my face! My eyes sparkle and my lips smile! I am happy in your very midst, because you have left me alone with him! This is what I wanted; this is my victory!

– Enough!

– Enough!

– You're a woman!

– Nothing but a female!

– That's your defense.

– That's your punishment!

– In the midst of all of them, I feel alone with you, as though we were in the middle of a desert! My love! Yes, at last I can say to you: I love you!

– You whore!

– Enough, by God, or I'll have the courtroom cleared!

– Silence!

211

– It was obvious how a woman's defense was going to end!

– Good God, what a scandal!

– I'm scared, I'm leaving.

– Scared of what?

– Don't go away, stay here, for heaven's sake.

– She has damaged all of us women in the worst way!

– After a beginning like that we're all done for.

– You've compromised all of us!

– Silence!

– Because of you, we shall never be able to aspire to the Courtroom.

– Silence!

– The punishment!

– Death!

– By water!

– Drown him!

– Put him with Iba!

– Put him back to roast over the fire!

– Put him under quicklime!

– You've got to bury him!

– Death!

– Here's Catulva!

– Catulva!

– The famous Catulva.

– She's come to the trial!

– Ask her what should be done!

– She knows all the secrets of the human heart.

– Madam, say something, speak!

– But one word, Madam!

– Of accusation or in defense!

– Yes.

– She said yes.

– She said: "yes."

– Yes how?
– Yes what?
– Is he innocent?
– Is he guilty?
– One goes...
– One goes where?
– When?
– How?
– With whom?
– Continue!
– Silence!
– That's all she says.
– Really too little.
– She doesn't know what to say, that's why!
– When they're not on the stage these actresses are quite stupid.
– All she can do is mince about.
– The punishment!
– Death!
– Death!
– That's easily said, but you'd have to know what to do in order to kill him.
– To Calleio!
– To Calleio!
– Death!
– With human flesh we have some experience by now, but with smoke...
– Prince Zarlino!
– Prince Zarlino?
– They've let the lunatics out!
– What will happen?
– Look, look, he's going up to the cage! He's stretching his arms out!
– They're embracing!
– Ooh!

– How sweet they are, the two of them!

– How cute!

– They've embraced like brothers.

Prince Zarlino is dressed in magnificent gray velvet, and he has smeared his face with some sort of lead-colored ointment. For three days he has been playing Perelà in the asylum.

– The punishment!

– Death!

– The Queen's messenger!

– Let him speak!

– We can't hear anything, damn it!

– The Queen is in her apartments pacing anxiously from room to room with her arms hanging limply, and all that can be heard now is one word: "God."

– Great personages are of few words.

– Few but effective.

– Long live the Queen!

– Down with the Marchesa di Bellonda!

– She invokes God. But anyone who in a human struggle invokes a power he considers greater than himself is a frightened weakling!

– It's not she who invokes Him, it's her parrot!

The Marchesa's voice is completely drowned out by a storm of boos.

– Can't you make her keep quiet?

– Shut that woman's mouth up!

– Pick her up and cart her away!

The Minister of Justice rises and prepares to read the verdict. As if by a magic spell, the courtroom falls into a silence that is terrifying.

– Inasmuch as the accused has, by a unanimous verdict, been found guilty, and inasmuch as any other form of punishment has been determined to be of doubtful efficacy, the Minister of Justice hereby sentences him to solitary confinement for life, while recognizing the absence of ways and means to establish the expectancy of that life...

– Coward!

– Take her away by force!

– Coward!

– What does it take to drag away a woman?

– Coward!

– Cut her tongue out!

– He will not be committed to an ordinary prison; rather, a special cell will be built for him atop Mount Calleio from whence he descended one day to bring disorder and ruin in our midst. There he will be immured.

– Vile!

– Bravo!

– Vile!

– Splendid!

– Buried alive!

– Long live the Minister!

– The King!

Now only the King can revoke the sentence and grant a pardon. His is the supreme judgment.

In the center of the wall, above the courtroom gallery, a large purple drape with gold fringes opens, and behind a thick glass appears the person of the King wearing his mantle and crown and holding a scepter in each hand: in the right hand that of Power, in the left hand that of Justice.

At this moment everyone holds his breath. The scene high above the courtroom absorbs everyone's attention. All that can be heard is the panting of a woman's heaving bosom.

– Up...up...up...

It's as though she were trying with body and soul to raise the Sovereign's hand. If he raises his right hand during the thirty-three seconds in which the door-curtain remains open, pardon is granted and the sentence annulled. If his right hand remains lowered, the sentence is irrevocably confirmed.

The seconds run into one another convulsively.

– Uu...p...uu...p...uu...p...uu...p...coward! You too, you're afraid!

– To the King!

– Listen to what she's saying to the King!

– She's his cousin.

– Tie her up!

– Have her tied up!

– The handcuffs!

– Isn't there anybody with a gun in his pocket to shoot that woman?

– Nobody can do anything to her.

– What a bunch of incompetents!

– Cowards, one worse than the other! I shall go to all the peoples of the earth to tell them how you condemned an innocent man. The courts of every realm shall know how such infamy was perpetrated! And you, Minister of lies, when you are asked to explain his condemnation, when you are asked what you did with that just one, what will you reply?

– That "just one" was no man, but merely a man of smoke.

– And how will you answer for the Marchesa Oliva di Bellonda?

– As of this moment the Marchesa di Bellonda is not responsible for her own actions!

– Fine....Well done, all of you....You have crushed me! I am...vanquished, undone, trod upon by all, and it is as one who is vanquished that I now speak to you. As one who has been vanquished, I may at least supplicate. Among a people with honor, the victor grants a request to the fallen.

– Speak.

– He will not ask for food in prison, as do all other prisoners. He will not ask even for a chair. Iba was granted all the wine he desired after his treasure was fraudulently seized. But you cannot forget that this man is the son of fire. This you cannot deny. I beseech the Court in its mercy to grant that his narrow cell have at least a fireplace, a little chimney, the chimney where he was born and where he always lived in happiness, nourished by fire and the voices of his foster-mothers. You need not bother to supply him with a single log. I... I will go to him every evening with firewood so that he may warm his stiffened limbs and revive his poor eyes in the cold of night. You will grant me this request that I ask of you...on my knees.

– Come, arise, arise, Marchesa. Your request is granted. His cell shall have the chimney you wish for him; and on the door we shall drill a hole, through which you will be able to hand him all the wood you desire, and through which you will be able to see your lover.

– Ooh!

– He's covered her with shame!

– That handful of mud was needed!

– She had it coming!

– Mud, shame, my dear friends? It wasn't long ago that Signor Perelà heard each of you pronounce the word "lover" in a free and easy manner.

– That's not true!

– Liar!

– She lied!

– You jade!

– None of you spoke of mud then and no one spoke of shame. The lover of whom I could not boast then – behold him! I boast of him now. Now you and I are alike.

– Shameless hussy!

– How brazen!

– Madwoman!

– Rotten bitch!

– Court is adjourned.

– Goodby, my dear Gelasia.

– *Adieu, mon ange.*

– Goodby, Zoë.

– What a madhouse!

– I feel thoroughly mixed up.

– I have a splitting headache.

– How awful!

– And to think that Oliva was the woman about whom nobody ever had anything to say.

– She's put herself on a par with the rest of us with one stroke.

– She really did.

– Still waters run deep.

– She seemed so gentle in her incurable melancholy.

– Such a meek creature.

– What a performance!

– She's gone crazy.

– This is some scandal.

– Not even Bianca Delle Catene in her cemetery caused such a commotion.

– And her poor husband?

– Who kept silent through it all.

– What was there for him to say, the poor devil.

– She'll turn their house into a lumberyard.

– And her husband into a lumberjack.

– When she goes by in her carriage the children yell after her; and this morning, when she came here, everyone said: "Here's Signora Perelà."

– She's become a laughingstock; she'll never get over this.

– Ha, ha!

– Are you coming to Nadina's tonight?

– Of course.

– We'll all be there.

– See you later, my dear.

– See you tonight.

– No one will be missing.

– That's certain.

– Ah! Yes, Signora Perelà!

– A real pity!

The Code of Perelà

Following the trial, Perelà is led back to the Royal Palace, where he is confined to his quarters and guarded by four sentries in full uniform. He is to remain there as long as it takes to build his cell on the top of Mount Calleio.

This generous act of the King and the Minister of Justice in taking him back under the Royal roof after he had been condemned has enraged and aroused the masses. The regard with which he continues to be treated is judged severely as bordering on the grotesque.

"Why such an excessively merciful attitude on the Sovereign's part? He should have been treated as all the others are, no better and no worse – in fact more harshly, much more harshly than the others! What guilty person cannot find a single word to justify or to attenuate his wrong? A word of regret capable of winning some indulgence? And yet he didn't find that word, indeed he didn't even take the trouble to look for it! What the devil were they preparing for him up there, a comfortable country-house in which to pass the approaching summer months? The judges have shown their partiality for this fellow quite unmistakably and right to the end." Such is the talk going around. "Criminals should be dealt with for what they are," they said. "Since when has anyone sentenced to life imprisonment been welcomed into the Palace and given the care and treatment reserved for princes of the Royal House? And the poor King who had run the gravest risk with that scoundrel in his residence still kept him attached to his person like a leech! A big fat-head, to put it mildly! Goodness has its limits, like everything else: to go beyond them is ill-advised, absurd! He held his arms out to him right up to the end! A prison just for him, built expressly for him, brand new! Now wasn't that a comical idea? Very comical indeed! What will they think of next? Don't be in a hurry to die, because there's something to be learned every day! Wouldn't it be something if henceforth for each of these charlatans we were to build a chalet in a lovely spot of their own choosing? Who wouldn't want to do something really bad? Before long our hills would become filled with chalets, and when we go out for a Sunday stroll with our families we'd have one of these bastards to go and visit. Besides breathing pure air, they'd be honored by endless pilgrimages, just like the Holy Father in Rome. Is it the rule of progress that's bringing new ways to punish criminals?"

There was only one good thing about the idea: in order to go from the Royal Palace to Calleio Gate (the ancient gate had resumed its legitimate name) the prisoner had to cross the city, going along the main streets, and he had to go on foot because hard criminals are not brought by carriage. Thus with the greatest convenience every citizen could hurl at him a last deadly insult – a shout, a gibe, a gesture of derision – and thereby do justice themselves, or delude themselves that they had, which is the same thing. It's an illusion that the people dearly love, and one that's quite easy to satisfy at will.

Everybody waited anxiously for that day.

The cubbyhole on the top of the mountain was built with the stones of Mount Calleio itself and was ready in short order. It was a cell six feet wide and six feet long, sunk into the ground and rising nine feet above it. At ground level there was a small door lined with iron-plate and nailed with huge spikes. In the upper part there was a small square aperture with two cross-bars, from which the inmate was to receive light and air and tiny pieces of firewood should someone bring any to him. A pitiless hovel such as had never before been constructed for anyone: the tomb of a living soul.

In looking through that aperture one had to adjust one's eyes to the darkness, and in order to make out anything within, not block it completely with one's face. The opposite wall was taken up by the fireplace, and on the roof there was the vertical tube from which smoke was to come out should the inmate obtain the means to produce it.

Mount Calleio is the highest summit in the hills surrounding the city. Not taller than fifteen hundred feet, its lower slopes are endowed with green trees and well-cultivated fields that lend it a lovely symmetrical pattern; but from midway on up vegetation is random and wild. The calcareous nature of the soil and the barrenness resulting from the rushing downflow of the rains prevent any cultivation, and the only things that grow there are the parasitic plants found in arid and sandy terrains. The mountain is crowned by a mass of stones that assume the appearance of ruins.

Flanked by cypresses paired like friars, a beautiful lane turns off the main road and climbs to the upper limit of the cultivated areas. From that point, to reach the summit one must follow a path that winds tortuously like a ribbon between the rocks.

The condemned man's cell is built on a level area of the summit. From up there one has a sweeping view of the entire city, which from a central basin of thickly settled dwellings gradually broadens, climbing and spreading over a long chain of hills that with unmatched grace form a royal crown around the city as far as the eye can see.

Since noon the streets along the route have been crowded. The Royal Square is crammed like a pomegranate, right up to the Palace railing, which is blocked by a cordon of soldiers who are there to keep the crowd back. At all the windows there is a great buzz of excitement. The houses are overflowing: relatives, friends – all those who, though not living along the route, have the good fortune of knowing somebody who does.

Perelà is to retrace the route he took the first day, when he arrived alone and unknown, the same one he travelled triumphantly on the evening when the people hailed him as a new Prophet.

The scheduled time is one o'clock, but it has already gone by without a sign of anything starting. All the windows of the Royal Palace are shut as though a funeral procession were to come from out the door.

And as inevitably happens in certain circumstances, conjectures begin to be made and quickly multiply, spreading with dizzying speed. In some situations it is essential that the awaited personage be late. For such an event to be successful, having the public wait is an indispensable, an absolute prerequisite; it lends the event a sense of importance and solemnity. The longer a King makes people wait, the more he is acclaimed by them. People do not intend to get tired for nothing, and to remain standing for a long time demands an adequate reward. And in the meanwhile they have the time to chatter until their throats are dry, time to get worked up and make one another excited until they've reached the limits of their imagination in a contest for which no amount of waiting is too long. If an important personage were to arrive five minutes too early, he would not have allowed for enough expectation and would accordingly be received with a general coldness and diffidence, as one who exploits an undeserved fame. Everybody would look upon him as an insignificant fellow who is stealing away in a hurry, full of concerns, a poor devil who, like numberless others, scratches around on the earth, who wants only to finish up his business, who has no time to waste – a sorry thing – and who, when taking out a watch from his vest pocket, smiles self-complacently in seeing that he is a few minutes ahead of his busy schedule – what rubbish – a person of absolutely no account and of no appeal.

In this particular case, the sense of expectation is increased by the curiosity, the contempt, and the hatred felt for the condemned man.

People begin to fear that the King has made a terrible blunder – it wouldn't be the first time – and has had Perelà taken away secretly during the night so as to save him from the righteous wrath of the crowd!

Of course, the King decided to spare him this embarrassment, favoring him to the end and thereby protecting himself from some surprise or other. One never knows about a mob on the move; fear is a mighty persuader. People are all right as long as they're in their homes – if they have one – and when they go on family outings on Sundays. "We'll be left here like so many pumpkins for someone who isn't going to show up, until we are told that nobody is coming because of 'this' because of 'that' – whatever they choose to say – all stuff that has been expressly planned so as not to tell us anything! The truth is eaten by those who cook it up, and they're careful not to leave a crumb of it fall! The King's weakness for that fine fellow is no laughing matter! And the Ministers, including the Minister of Justice, have treated him with a deference that makes your stomach turn! There must be something pretty fishy behind all this that we don't know about and that no one will ever find out. And that's no lie!" Such a way of doing things exasperates peaceful people, just imagine the others. Yet everyone uses the same weapon – one's tongue. It's fast approaching two o'clock...the square is an immense snorting locomotive...

Rataplan...Rataplan...Rataplan...Rataplan plan plan.
Rataplan...Rataplan...Rataplan...Rataplan plan plan.
Dun...Dun...Dun...Dun...Dun...Dun...

The sentries at the main door of the Palace draw back, and the first two drummers come forth twelve feet apart. Then comes Perelà. Behind him are two more drummers who with the first two form a square. In the center the condemned man walks briskly, almost rising from the ground with each step he takes, while the procession forms and moves ahead gravely, slowly, at a funereal pace. There follow, twelve feet behind one another, four rows of soldiers swinging their rifles.

Drums rolling, the procession descends the great outer staircase of the Palace with heavy tread. Only Perelà seems to raise himself on each step as though to take flight and complete the rest of the staircase with one leap, so light is his gait. He crosses the garden, goes beyond the iron railing, and is in the square.

From the prison-house at the other end of the city, the bell cleaves the dense atmosphere with its torpedoes of death headed toward the condemned man.

Dun…Dun…Dun…Dun…Dun…Dun…

The Palace square swells and seethes in a general tumult. Like rockets the first shouts begin to be launched – invectives, insults, hoots.

The procession is on level ground and moves up the main avenue of the city. The sidewalks and windows crammed with heads seem like the stalls on which the market-gardeners display turnips, onions, and beets. At the windows of the Royal Palace a few heads peep out from behind the closed shutters.

The main avenue is now criss-crossed by shouts and cries that intertwine from window to window like unravelling streamers. From a window a large blob of spit comes down – splat! – and plops at the feet of the condemned man. Perelà doesn't turn, nor does he give signs of having seen it. But when the example is quickly followed, the four drummers move over to the sides near the crowd of onlookers among whom a hurly-burly ensues in the effort to avoid the jetsam, leaving the prisoner in the center as the sole target. And then another blob, another, and yet another while the crowd begins to flee and

the drummers move more and more to the sides so
as not to be covered with spit.

*Squish! Squoosh! Chak! Krscht! Krshplat!
Krchak!*

From all the windows the spittle rains down like
arrows – snowflakes, egg-whites and glass pellets
somersaulting through the air like tiny batons of
mercury. Everyone has stopped shouting in order to
vent their scorn in this way, and many keep a
lozenge in their mouths to spit the better.

Men have invented complex and refined devices
for all the manifestations of life, but when they
wish to express their deepest feelings they still
have recourse to the innermost substance within
their bodies, to what they consider to be the foulest
matter of all.

At Calleio Gate a crowd waits to follow the
procession. A carriage stands motionless with its
curtains drawn closed. Perelà passes in the middle
of four drummers who have returned to their
positions.

*Rataplan...Rataplan...Rataplan...Rataplan plan
plan.*

The curtain of the carriage opens slightly and a
flashing glimpse of a white face is seen.

The drummers with their beating, the four rows
of soldiers, and several hundred persons thronging
behind them. Finally, a closed black carriage covered and dripping with spittle advances very slowly
as if following a funeral cortège.

Dun...Dun...Dun...Dun...Dun...Dun...

The throng of people becomes thinner and thinner. As the procession moves farther away from the
city, many halt and, finally satisfied, turn back.

We are at the beginning of the cypress-flanked lane that leads to the climb of Mount Calleio. In the rear are no more than a hundred persons and the closed carriage.

We are at the end of the lane where the rocky path begins. Most of the remaining crowd halt and linger to look from below at the ascent of the last stretch. The carriage also halts, and the Marchesa Oliva di Bellonda steps down.

Up and up along the steep, rocky mountain slope go Perelà, the drummers, the soldiers, and a pack of obstinate followers, about fifty or so – the most inexorable and indefatigable hurlers of insults, with livid faces and hoarse voices. Behind them all, the woman drags her black mantle up the arduous ascent. Below is the group of those who stayed to observe until the end, their bodies contracted and their mouths agape like ransacked strong-boxes.

Perelà is shut up in his cell irreparably.

The soldiers, the drummers, and the jailer with the fatal key go back down; and after them the pack of obstinate followers descends with a last ugly and satisfied look, their final wordless insult – the most deadly. The woman who has stayed alone and apart now approaches a living man's tomb, which she encircles two, three times. She stops at the small aperture and remains fixed there for a long time, peering inside without saying anything. The man, now no more than a shadow in that darkness, stands beneath the chimney cowl. Tall, calm, serene, he seems to set himself there like the figure of a nobleman in a painting.

"He must be cold," she thinks; "tomorrow... tomorrow when I come,..." but she says nothing.

And he looks at her in turn, without the strength to exchange a word or to shape his lips into a smile.

The soldiers, with the followers behind them, descend the slope with the gait of someone returning after having performed a duty. Left alone on the summit, the woman too begins the descent, moving with unsteady and weary step until she reaches the waiting carriage.

The sun is setting. The disk is a fiery host atop the opposite mountain, a pure host of light and heat. Down amid the rocks of Mount Calleio, the black figure becomes smaller and smaller – a pure host of love and sorrow.

The sun has disappeared behind the mountain. The woman climbs into her carriage, and the horses go off at a trot.

"I stand under this chimney and look up at the little blue disk. That blue belongs to me because it was created by love. In this beautiful sunset I leave my last wishes. My feet are joined and my boots stand side by side as they did that day when I struggled down to them. I leave them that way, exactly as you had prepared them for me. *Pena! Rete! Lama!* You gave me these boots that I might walk on this earth among men, I know. And perhaps I ought to have walked until they were worn out. If men had always made me walk as they did today, I could now leave a pair of ruined boots down here; but because men made me travel in splendid, comfortable carriages and because there was always someone who took care to clean and polish these boots every morning, they are still in perfect condition, as beautiful and shiny as when you gave them to me, and the soles are still like new. These

are everything that I own and all that I can leave to
you, oh men; they are what bound me to you. Thus
you will know what I was really worth. I was worth
this pair of boots that I leave here – you may have
them. You called me by the most flattering names
and you bowed deeply and reverently to me. You
worshipped me as one worships the holy relics and
the saints on your altars. Then you realized that I
was not worth much, that I was not worth anything.
And so you despised me, crushed me underfoot like
some poisonous reptile, covered me with insults as
you would a thief or a murderer, and you sent me far
from you – banished forever, confined – so that you
could forget me. You wanted so much from me –
that I prescribe a Code. Well then, here it is. Only
these boots could be the Code of one whom you
chose to call Perelà. I bequeath them to you. They
alone could anchor to earth my one and only virtue.
In this beautiful sunset will rise a small gray cloud
in the shape of a man – clouds may take all shapes;
upward and onward it will cross the sky, beyond
the horizon, beyond the sun, into infinity. It will go
unnoticed, or if anyone does happen to notice it he
will smile at its diminutive grace without knowing
what it is. Except perhaps a poor woman who will
give her last sob for me. To her go all my thoughts
in this moment, though even she could not understand that my heart also was of smoke and that I
was only light...so light...so light...so light.

While his legs are coming out of the boots, a
pink cardboard disk, his pass, falls to the ground,
and the man's last look rests on the last earthly
word – *"et ultra."*

– Hear me! Come! Run! Cowards! Run, all of you! Run with me!
– The Marchesa di Bellonda!
– She's gone crazy!
– Listen! Up there!...in the cell...Perelà...he is no longer there! I went to bring him firewood for the night...he is no longer there...the cell is empty...and under the chimney only his boots remain!
– Has he run away?
– No, he has flown!
– Where?
– How?
– When?
– Up into the sky!
– Madwoman!
– Look at her, she's going berserk!
– She's already berserk!
– Mangy curs!
– Grab her!
– Scoundrels!
– She's delirious!
– Murderers!
– She's crazy!
– He has flown...
– She's crazy!
– Up into the sky!
– She's crazy!
– Follow me...follow me...come...let us go...let us go to tell...to tell so as to kill...we must tell... we must ki...Aah!
– She's crazy!
– Grab her! She's fallen into a fit!
– No! Don't go near her...she's fallen dead. She ran too hard....Poor woman. Her heart burst.

231

His Lightness Perelà

– How streaked the sky is today! It looks like a new breed of new men, doesn't it?
– No, rather of new birds.
– Look, everybody! Look!
– Look at what's up there in the sky!
– Make me fly, love!
– White eagles, eagles white as swans, gold eagles, silver eagles, black eagles, eagles of all colors are flying up, straight up, with their hooked beaks, up and up into the sky.
– They're going up to God to tear away the veil of His mystery!
– Nonsense!
– Those flags way up there...they're going up to slap the blue with the blood of their victory!
– Nonsense!
– How streaked the sky is today!
– Make me fly, love!
– Those men are going up to deliver their souls to God with their own hands!
– Nonsense!
– Where are they going?
– They're going to look for Perelà.
– Perelà?
– Signor Perelà?
– Ha! Ha! Ha! Ha!

Florence, 1908-1910

232

This Book Was Completed on February 9, 1992 at Italica Press, New York, New York and Was Set in Galliard. It Was Printed on 50 lb Glatfelter Natural Acid-Free Paper with a Smyth-Sewn Binding by McNaughton & Gunn, Ann Arbor, MI U. S. A.

* *

*